GALAXIES

BARRY N. MALZBERG

GALAXIES

FOREWORD BY JACK DANN

AØP
ANTI-OEDIPUS PRESS

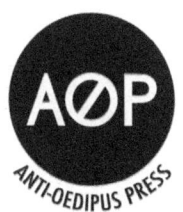

PRAISE FOR BARRY N. MALZBERG

"There are possibly a dozen genius writers in the genre of the imaginative, and Barry Malzberg is at least eight of them."
—Harlan Ellison

"Malzberg makes persuasively clear that the best of science fiction should be valued as literature and nothing else."
—The Washington Post

"One of the finest practitioners of science fiction."
—Harry Harrison

"Barry N. Malzberg's writing is unparalleled in its intensity and in its apocalyptic sensibility. His detractors consider him bleakly monotonous and despairing, but he is a master of black humor, and is one of the few writers to have used science fiction's vocabulary of ideas extensively as apparatus in psychological landscapes, dramatizing relationships between the human mind and its social environment in an SF theater of the absurd."
—The Encyclopedia of Science Fiction

"The writer who attempts to use the SF mythos as Malzberg has is bedevilled by the inappropriateness of the 'rules' pertaining to the production and consumption of mass-produced fiction."
—Brian Stableford

"Malzberg is a true hero."
—The Magazine of Fantasy & Science Fiction

"There is no one, with the possible exception of Philip K. Dick, whose works, each one of them, are so unpredictable or so outrageous and outraged."
—Theodore Sturgeon

"Barry Malzberg is one of science fiction's most literate and erudite writers."
—New York Times Book Review

Galaxies
Copyright © 1975 by Barry N. Malzberg
ISBN: 978-0-98-923914-1
Library of Congress Control Number: 2014933477

First published in the United States by Pyramid Books

First Anti-Oedipal Paperback Edition: March 2014

www.rawdogscreaming.com

"Two Forwards for the Price of One" © 2014 by Jack Dann. "Forward to the 1998 Edition" © 1997 by Jack Dann. First published in *Three in Space* in 1998. Reprinted by permission of the author.

Cover Design by Matthew Revert
www.matthewrevert.com

Interior Layout by D. Harlan Wilson
www.dharlanwilson.com

Anti-Oedipus Press
Grand Rapids, MI

www.anti-oedipuspress.com

ALSO BY BARRY N. MALZBERG

NOVELS

FICTION COLLECTIONS

Out from Ganymede
The Many Worlds of Barry Malzberg
Down Here in the Dream Quarter
The Best of Barry Malzberg
Malzberg at Large
The Man Who Loved the Midnight Lady
The Passage of the Light
In the Stone House
On Account of Darkness and Other SF Stories
The Very Best of Barry N. Malzberg

NONFICTION

The Engines of the Night
Breakfast in the Ruins
The Business of Science Fiction

First the corpus, then the mind, the consciousness, then self-awareness and its extensions: the environment, the abstract environment, immortality, matters of the spirit. We can assume a continuity of these qualities and we can even assume that that which would insist upon imposing order would continue to do so even after the point of physical death. But in order to be completely secure with these assumptions we would have to define some terms. What is "consciousness" or the "spirit"? What is "order"? For that matter, what is "physical death"?

—H.H. Brenner, *The Last Possessor*

TWO FOREWORDS FOR THE PRICE OF ONE

Jack Dann

FOREWORD TO THE 2014 EDITION

Who the hell is this writer Barry Malzberg?

Mainstream critics (and I use that word loosely) can't seem to make him out. They don't know where to put him. They hate him. They love him. They think he's a great artist. They think he's a hack. They are as bewildered as Dorothy upon discovering that they're not in Kansas anymore.

This from J. D. Daniels in a recent issue of *The Paris Review*:

> I love Barry Malzberg, in my own way. Anyone can see that.
> I have read many of his novels, several of them more than
> once, in order to construct the authority I felt I needed to
> make these remarks. If that isn't love—or is it only obses-
> sion: I read *Beyond Apollo* seven times, and retyped almost

all of it to get it into my working memory before a friend convinced me that would not be necessary.

And then . . .

I aim to condescend to Malzberg and repudiate him, but not to such an extent that I must cast him off with utter finality, because I still love him and want him somewhere near me—"in town and out of my sight," as Jack Lipnik said to Barton Fink—and that, I think, is an ugly trick to play on him. Make no mistake, I do not want you to read him. I wouldn't wish that on my worst enemy: myself. Malzberg is an unsuitable love object, and he's all mine. I love him, all right, but as my friend Donna used to say: Everything that looks good to you ain't good for you.

Yeah, we get that you love him and hate him and don't get him.

J. D. Daniels' reaction has been par for the course for Malzberg. Either his work has gone unappreciated (until recently!) or the work and his considerable presence have been met with controversy, dismay, and antagonism. For example, when *Beyond Apollo* won the very first John W. Campbell Memorial Award for Best Novel in 1973, there was a great hue and cry from many in the science fiction community because it wasn't the "right" sort of science fiction. Robert Shaw denounced the book as "the epitome of everything that has gone wrong with SF in the last ten years" while Harlan Ellison praised it and said that it "put me out of commission for three days after reading it."

*

The novel you are about to read might not put you out of commission for three days (well, maybe it will!), but it is a masterpiece—and you won't need a degree in gonzo journalism to "get it." *Galaxies* will suck you right in (all various and sundry puns on black holes intended). It will transform you, like it or not, into a literary collaborator. And you'll feel like you're flying over the Himalayas on a combination of amphetamines and hallucinogens. It's a postmodern postmodernist's novel. It's a genre science fiction novel with bells on. It's a mainstream experiment with science fiction tropes. It's a nonfiction handbook on the craft of writing. It's a writer's diary, an impenitent memoir. It's Steinbeck's *Journal of a Novel* and Hemingway's *A Moveable Feast* told from the perspectives of the (impossibly) tangled present and a(n impossibly) schizoid future. It's a deconstruction à la Derrida, Foucault, and Lyotard. And, yes—and this is the biggest "and"—it's easy to read: no muzzy denseness, no literary obfuscation, no fatuous polemic.

That's a lot of weight for 65,000 words of masterpiece to carry, and my suggestion is that you skip all my ranting and praising and go directly to the first page of the main text. The novel tells it all: I've just been invited to do a bit of a tap dance because I had some glancing involvement in the initial creation of *Galaxies* . . . but I'm about as necessary here as a cummerbund in a nudist camp.

After you've read the novel—and should you be so disposed—come back and I'll tell you why writers shouldn't throw stones. And I'll give you some background on the author of this brilliant, unique work of literature.

*

Galaxies began as a story entitled "A Galaxy Called Rome," which was published by the perspicacious publisher of *The Magazine of Fantasy & Science Fiction* in 1975. George Zebrowski and I were editing an anthology entitled *Faster Than*

Light for Harper & Row, and we asked Barry for a story. George sent him a fistful of material on black holes and seemingly by return mail (Malzberg was and is *fast*), we received "A Galaxy Called Rome." We thought it was absolutely brilliant, but came to the conclusion that it did not "fit" the hard science requirements of our anthology. Oh, man, did I get that one wrong! That was the equivalent of John Campbell refusing to serialize Joe Haldeman's *The Forever War* in *Analog* because it depicted men and women fighting side by side. "A Galaxy Called Rome" had multiple prestige reprints and expanded as the novel *Galaxies* was shortlisted for the Nebula Award and included in David Pringle's *Science Fiction: The 100 Best Novels*.

So I guess I'd better go easy on J. D. Daniels . . .

I was, however, able to reprint *Galaxies* in 1998. A small expiation, but expiation nevertheless. The anthology was called *Three in Space*, and was edited by George Zebrowski, Pam Sargent, and myself. (We jointly determined all the selections.) I'm including my forward to that edition. It is of its time, but I think it does give some insight into the man and his work.

I wrote then that Malzberg's work is difficult to find and awaits discovery.

Well, it's 2014, and Malzberg has been discovered with a vengeance. (Take a look at www.beyondapollo.com for information on a film adaptation of *Beyond Apollo*, which will star Bill Pullman, Scott Speedman, and Ali Larter. Funding has been secured, and the project is, as they say, in development.)

Hallelujah!

*

If I were a more pedantic and patient introducer, I would try to summarize in bibliographical fashion his impressive oeuvre. But it's easy to find Malzberg bibliographies on the Internet, so

I'll spare you the lists. As a first stop, I would suggest taking a look at his entry in the definitive online version of *The Encyclopedia of Science Fiction*. Like Bob Silverberg, Barry is a prolific genius. One might say he's the Joyce Carol Oates of science fiction. I am, of course, being facetious; but there is a nugget of truth in the pie. Just as there is a nugget of truth in Jeffrey M. Wallman's contention in the *St. James Guide to Science Fiction Writers* that "*Galaxies* reaches areas that formerly were reserved to philosophical speculation and that remind the reader vividly of fiction by Pynchon and Borges."

Well, nah . . .

Malzberg reminds me of only one writer: Barry N. Malzberg.

FOREWORD TO THE 1998 EDITION

It's 1994, and I've just arrived at the Sky Garden Room of the St. Moritz Hotel on Central Park. I'm standing cheek-to-jowl with a clutch of writers, editors, publishers, and agents; it's the annual Science Fiction Writers of America Authors-Editors Reception, and it's a cold Monday night in November. But it's warm and close in this room at the top of New York. Writers are cruising around, looking fresh and intent, drinks in hand, searching for editors to "do business with," while most of the editors are standing around in rumpled suits, being polite, putting in the requisite appearance after a heavy day's work in the office. The views from the balconies are breathtaking: New York City in all its splendor, clouds and avenues of Christmas lights, and from this height, Manhattan Island takes on the outline of a great ship cruising through the darkness.

I look around for Barry N. Malzberg. He promised to meet me here.

I push through the crowd and slowly make my way across the room. I talk with old friends, do a little business, shake hands, and then I hear a deep, low voice, a voice that somehow combines humor and resignation and absolute finality—"Hello, Jack." I turn around, and there he is beside me, thin and hunched over and looking uncomfortable and miserable in a black suit. He's taller than anyone else in the room, a stork standing among the penguins. "You're late. I've been here for ninety minutes."

We talk and try to catch up, for we've known each other for a lifetime; but Barry grows more uncomfortable and more nervous with every second, as if he's trapped and doing all he can to hold back the panic and, perhaps, revulsion; and finally he says, "This is it, Jack, an hour and a half is my limit, that's all I can take, I'm out of it, out of it, it's over for me, I'm sorry, I wanted to see you, but"—he glances quickly around the room and says, "Why do we do this to ourselves?" and then he bolts for the door.

I follow him to the elevators.

As the elevator doors close, we stare at each other.

Goodbye, Barry . . .

He will calm down in the cool darkness of a concert hall where he will lose himself in Mahler or Berlioz or Bach; and as I walk back into the humid, noisy room, into the comforting swell of dear friends and old acquaintances, I imagine him striding down the streets alone.

Barry . . . the quintessential outsider.

*

Over a period of four decades, Barry N. Malzberg has written mainstream fiction, erotic fiction, and mystery and suspense, but his considerable reputation rests on his science fiction novels and short stories. He is the author of over seventy novels and over two hundred short stories; some of his short fiction may be found in the collections *Final War and Other Fantasies* (as K. M. O'Donnell, 1969), *In the Pocket and Other Science Fiction Stories* (as K. M. O'Donnell, 1971), *Out From Ganymede* (1974), *The Many Worlds of Barry Malzberg* (1975), *Down Here in the Dream Quarter* (1976), *The Best of Barry Malzberg* (1976), *Malzberg at Large* (1979), *The Man Who Loved the Midnight Lady* (1980), and *The Passage of the Night: The Recursive Science Fiction of Barry N. Malzberg* (1994).

Malzberg began as a playwright, but turned to writing science fiction consistently and prolifically for about seven years after his first sale to Fred Pohl at *Galaxy Magazine*. The story was "We're Coming through the Windows" and it appeared in the August 1967 issue. But it was his second story that established him as an innovator who would come to exemplify the literary experimentation and questioning of traditional values that was associated with the New Wave movement of the late sixties and early seventies. "Final War" was a dark and caustic reflection on war as a game that never ends; it was published in the April 1968 issue of *The Magazine of Fantasy & Science Fiction*.

Malzberg's earliest novel of note was *Oracle of the Thousand Hands* (1968), which was published by the controversial Olympia Press. He wrote nine other novels for Olympia, including *Screen* (1970), *In My Parents' Bedroom* (1970), and *Confessions of Westchester County* (1971). As Malzberg writes in his autobiographical sketch in Contemporary Authors:

"You son of a bitch," Maurice Girodias said to me in a restaurant, a week after I had delivered *Screen* to his Olympia Press . . . "You son of a bitch, you give me literature, you give me horse racing and decadence and death and impotence and darkness! So I have, you see, no nice little book of porno-graffee as I wish; I have this literature.

I cannot publish it in paperback, of course; they would throw it across the room. I publish in hardcover then, and I lose all my money."

In 1969, Malzberg began publishing science fiction under the pseudonym K. M. O'Donnell.* Besides the two pseudonymous short story collections mentioned above, he wrote the novels *The Empty People* (1969), *Dwellers of the Deep* (1970), *Universe Day* (1971), and *Gather in the Hall of the Planets* (1971). His first SF novel under his own name was *The Falling Astronauts* (1971), which was followed by *Beyond Apollo* (1972). This controversial novel about the first manned expedition to Venus is narrated by the only survivor of the mission, who is probably insane. Robert Silverberg wrote that "Barry Malzberg's dark, bleak vision of the future is one of the most terrifying ever to come out of science fiction." When *Beyond Apollo* won the first John W. Campbell Jr. Memorial Award, traditional science fiction fans were incensed: this was *not* the kind of science fiction that the editor of *Astounding Stories* (later *Analog Science Fiction*) would have ever bought.

Beyond Apollo established Malzberg as a major science fiction writer.

Malzberg's most prolific period was during the 70's when he produced some of his most brilliant work, which would include the aforementioned *Beyond Apollo*, *Overlay* (1972), *The Men Inside* (1973), *Herovit's World* (1973), *The Destruction of the Temple* (1974), *Underlay* (1974), *Guernica Night* (1974), *Chorale* (1978), and *Galaxies* (1975). If I had to choose only the very best of Malzberg's work at novel length, it would have to be *Beyond Apollo*, *Herovit's World*, *Guernica Night*,

---

* Malzberg has written under a number of pseudonyms, which include Mike Barry, Francine de Natale, Claudine Dumas, Mel Johnson, Lee W. Mason, and Gerrold Watkins.

Galaxies, which is included here, and his last published novel *The Remaking of Sigmund Freud* (1985).

Barry Malzberg has also edited a number of important anthologies, which include the groundbreaking *Final Stage: The Ultimate Science Fiction Anthology* (with Edward L. Ferman, 1974, 1975), *The Arbor House Treasury of Horror and the Supernatural* (with Bill Pronzini and Martin H. Greenberg, 1981), and *The Arbor House Treasury of Mystery and Suspense* (with Bill Pronzini and Martin H. Greenberg, 1981).

I should also mention and recommend Malzberg's dark retrospective volume *The Engines of the Night* (1982), which won the Locus Award for nonfiction and was a Hugo Award finalist. It is one of the most important personal histories in the genre. When the book was published, writer, editor, and critic Algis Budrys wrote: "Destined to be misunderstood and mis-used, this cry from the heart will prove once more that honesty is suicidal."

∗

Barry's pain and revelation and genius have had a profound impact on science fiction, yet his dark, stabbing, autobiographical work has not received nearly the attention it deserves. Almost all of his titles are out of print; and now, at the very height of his powers, he has almost stopped writing.

How did this happen to the author who wrote *Herovit's World, Overlay, Guernica Night, The Remaking of Sigmund Freud, Beyond Apollo, Down Here in the Dream Quarter, The Engines of the Night,* and *Galaxies*?

One answer might be that Malzberg had no business being a genre writer. As a writer and editor once remarked, "Only Barry would try to become a commercially successful science fiction writer by grinding out great quantities of depressing science fiction novels and stories." And, indeed, Malzberg has more in common with writers such as Gogol, Kafka, and Rilke, or modern writers such as Barth, Barthelme, Bellows, Pynchon, and Oates. In a different timeline, in some alternate world, Barry N. Malzberg is having a career like the prolific Joyce Carol Oates, whose dark, alienated, internalized fiction has earned her a place in the current pantheon of literary lions. But whereas Oates (who admires Malzberg's work) directs some of her large output into the genre magazines and anthologies, Malzberg has never crossed over into the literary market.

In a candid interview with Charles Platt, he said:

> I became a science-fiction writer because I failed in my attempts to succeed in the literary world. I quit the largest writing fellowship in the country—the Cornelia Award Creative Writing Fellowship—in 1965 because I was being rejected. I was writing literary short stories and drowning in rejections and I just did not want to go any further.
>
> In October or November of that year I read in *Galaxy Magazine* Norman Kagan's story "Laugh Along with Franz." It was a brilliant, savage piece of science fiction, except it wasn't science fiction at all, it was a serious, savage work of American fiction by a young American fiction writer. I shook my head as I read it and I cynically said to myself, if this son of a bitch can get away with this kind of stuff in the commercial science fiction genre then I've got a future because I can do this just as well myself right now, and I can do it a little better in a couple of years, given a little training. If he can get away with this, I can too. And it was at that moment that I knew, viscerally, that I could sell science fiction.

If Malzberg had been patient . . . if he had kept sending out his work to the commercial markets . . . if he had kept writing plays . . . if he had submitted short stories to the literary quarterlies, which he didn't want to be in because "nobody read them and they didn't pay, so why bother" . . . would he have broken through to the literary mainstream firmament? Perhaps. Probably. But Barry Malzberg isn't patient. He paces around his home and office like a trapped animal and transforms his high anxiety into fiction, into diabolically self-referential and obsessive metafiction, postmodern fiction, humor, and autobiography. Although he now works on a computer, he used to type on an old portable Smith Corona manual, and he'd punch at those keys like a boxer going for a knockout.

He has written some of the darkest fiction in the genre, so dark that once the shock wears off, we realize we've been reading comedy by a master.

But is it *really* science fiction?

Malzberg uses the tropes of science fiction to catalogue his own inadequacies (and, by extension, our own) and—as Brian Stableford has said—to dramatize "relationships between the human mind and its social environment in an SF theatre of the absurd." His fiction is also profoundly political, but as critic Jeffrey M. Wallmann has written: "To say that . . . Malzberg is criticizing meaningless bureaucracy and arbitrary government in general, and the space program and space colonization in particular, may be correct but too easy. By leaving riddles unresolved at the end, and by rejecting the tenet that the aim of space travel is primarily pragmatic, Malzberg abandons a cornerstone of science fiction: the leading to a confirmation, not to a questioning, of the concept of reality and identity."

It has often been suggested that Malzberg's work isn't science fiction so much as postmodern fiction—a category that is as difficult to define as science fiction and would include fiction that "resists the very idea of boundaries," "regards distinctions as undesirable and even impossible," and "adopts a self-conscious intertextuality sometimes verging on pastiche, which denies the formal propriety of authorship and genre," to quote from *The Prentice Hall Guide to English Literature*.

If you are fortunate enough to find a copy of *The Engines of the Night* in a second-hand bookstore, flip to the last chapter entitled "Corridors." Is it an essay disguised as a short story, or a short story disguised as an essay? Is it autobiography or pastiche? For that matter is *Galaxies* a novel or an essay on the process of writing a novel with fictional episodes as illustration?

*

The first incarnation of *Galaxies* was a novelette called "A Galaxy Called Rome," which was originally published in *The Magazine of Fantasy & Science Fiction* in July 1975. It was reprinted a year later in his short story collection *Down Here in the Dream Quarter*. In the afterword to the story, Malzberg wrote:

> Here I address an old (maybe the oldest) question in our tortured category which will never be resolved: *what is science fiction?* And if we can ever define it, does it "mean" anything in the sense that commercial and literary fiction which deals with objective verifiable fact can be said to "mean" if not precisely "be"? Is science fiction merely another slightly distorted paradigm of common reality or is it something else which, at its best, can mysteriously assume the reality of a future we will never have?
>
> Difficult questions but I think that some tentative answers are here. I believe that good fiction can unfold its truths only on its own terms, that it cannot be paraphrased in terms other than its own and that the answers

cannot be adequately summarized. But perhaps there are given some suggestions.

When *Galaxies* was published in 1975, the reviews were few; but the one by Robert Silverberg is for the ages, since it confronts issues in the writing of science fiction that will not go away:

What Malzberg tells us, on every page, is that neither he nor Heinlein nor Doc Smith nor anybody can convey the reality of what it is like to be the pilot of a fortieth-century spaceship bearing a cargo of dead souls that is toppling into a black hole. It is audacious enough, says Malzberg, for a writer to think that he can show us the reality of a middle class New Jersey suburb in our own time; how then to handle all these unfathomable cosmic wonders? He can't. Yet he is a science fiction writer, and he must try. So try he does, magnificently, approaching his inconceivable thematic matter elliptically, obliquely, poking at it, toying with it, trying to seduce it into plausibility. Conventional science fiction novels of the kind this is packaged to look like bang straightforwardly away at their themes—hero, villain, problem, conflict, obstacles, complication, resolution—and if we have not lost the knack of willing suspension of disbelief we accept what their authors are saying, at least for the nonce. Malzberg can no longer suspend his own disbelief, and yet, oddly, as he wrestles with his impossibly grandiose conceptual burden of black holes and tachyonic drives, he achieves a kind of acceptance in the reader anyway. He persuades us, somehow, to glimpse the fortieth century. Of all his many novels, this is, I think, the most completely realized work of art, the most moving, the most profound, and despite its ostensible refusal to handle its material straightforwardly, the most successful work of science fiction he has produced.

Of course, I've lived on into the fourth generation myself, both as a reader and a writer, and my reaction to *Galaxies* may well be colored by my own accumulated troubles. Be warned by that confession of bias. *Galaxies* will probably not please the new reader of science fiction, the undemanding one, or the unsophisticated one. I think it will amaze and delight those who have grown and deepened since the days of Blackie Duquesne and Giles Habibula, and that it will altogether flabbergast the current generation of s-f writers who will find their private struggles to make sense out of the unimaginable laid bare here in an unforgettable manner.

✳

Whatever you might think of Malzberg's oeuvre—whatever you might think it is, or what it means, or what it means to accomplish—you should know that Barry N. Malzberg walked into all this with his eyes open. He chose his own way and disregarded the consequences. He didn't cave in to the demands of the market. He became the prince of the remainder bookshelf and the Cassandra of the genre. He wrote reams, for he's an extraordinarily prolific writer, and he thought, wrongly, that if he wrote a lot of fiction, even if it was uncompromisingly dark, he'd be able to make a good middle class living.

It worked . . . for a few glorious, prosperous years.

He had the house in the 'burbs and the great symbol of the 60's middle class: the Cadillac.

"A 1973 Calais Coup. Burnt Sienna. $6,500.00 plus tax."

He still has the house in the 'burbs . . . and he can still write fiction that is as brilliant and disconcerting and uncomfortable as anything he ever wrote in his salad days of the seventies and eighties. While most fiction reinforces our values, prejudices, and beliefs, Malzberg's work still makes us uncomfortable about everything we take for granted. His new work—what little there is of it—is still uncomfortable and sometimes revelatory. It is still bleak and funny and contradictory . . . and new. And the humor is still black as the pit at midnight.

But, as he once remarked, "I just won't keep throwing the work into a black hole." He recently wrote: "We learn and we learn and our knowledge reduces us to silence. (Or ascends to silence like the dead or the Just.)"

Certainly, to this reader, none of it has been in vain. The work remains, even if we must excavate the dark recesses of second-hand bookstores to find it. And in recent years, something has occurred that has even surprised Malzberg: he has become the acknowledged conscience of the genre.

For almost thirty years he told it like it was.

He didn't lie to us . . . or bullshit us. We found that all out later.

And it's all there in the fiction . . . and in the life.

The work only awaits rediscovery.

Melbourne, Australia
13 May 1997

I

To define terms at the outset, this will not be a novel so much as a series of notes toward one. Nevertheless pay attention, for it will cease to become a novel exactly at the point where it seems to be at last gathering force. Up until that time (which I will never tell), it will be as much of a novel as *The Rammers of Arcturus* or *Slinking Slowly on the Slime Planet's Sludge*, titles which flank this to left and right with covers offering inducements—let me be honest about this—they will never fulfill.

The novel itself cannot be written, at least by this writer, nor can it be encompassed by any techniques currently available, because it partakes of its time and that time is of the fortieth century, a time unimaginably distant . . . and it could be perceived only through the idiom and devices of that era which, to be sure, will not exist for more than eighteen hundred years.

Nor—continuing to be straightforward—will that idiom or those devices ever exist because science fiction is not a series of working models for the future but merely a subgenre of romantic fiction which employs the future as historicals would use the past, as Westerns would use the West, as pornography would use fornication—in short as a convention, which is the focus of their appeal. By virtue of these reasons, then, not to say others which are more personal—but which will be revealed— these fifty-five thousand words are little more than a set of constructions toward a construction even less substantial. It, as the writer himself, will not be finished in this world.

II

Let us talk about the writer a little if I may. Writers are not machines, you know, or disembodied personae, part of the printers' workshops: we have our qualities, we are people, we suffer, we *hurt*, although not as much, perhaps, as we would like you to believe. Still the writer is entitled to some explication. As he writes this novel he has slid past his thirty-fifth birthday and now confronts the not-distant monument of his thirty-sixth with bewilderment. Thirty-five is practically more than he can handle. He knows that forty is bad and fifty is worse, he has heard grim reports from even further on, but the writer has always thought of himself as being such a *young* man and ever-youthful; he has lurched through twenty-one, twenty-five, thirty years and similar landmarks in his shambling way, but nothing, either inherited or anticipated, has quite prepared him for the understanding that by Biblical calculation—by calculation, too, of much heredity—his life is fully at the halfway point. How can this be? The writer for many years was always the youngest person in the class. He finds his state hard to reckon with and he does not know with whom he can commiserate. Those older think he is young; those younger think he is old; his contemporaries have similar difficulties. Psychoanalysis is expensive and the writer has never had much faith in it.

The writer has struggled to order his life just as he is struggling now to order his sequence of notes for a novel entitled *Galaxies*, and yet no less than the wild and wonderful concepts which are surely to follow, he wonders whether he is really under control or whether it matters at all how he contemplates his death. His passage would be of little more consequence than his birth, which did not by much antedate the rape of Poland. Were the two somehow causally linked? Did the writer by being born cause Warsaw to be sealed off, reports moving toward the front lines on fine and invisible connection? Did he, by being born, cause the world to exist and by dying will he end it? This is the kind of megalomania with which he must deal—and yet it is this megalomania which is the key—God help him—to fiction which itself creates or manipulates worlds.

III

The reader may sit tight, however. The author is not a character in *Galaxies*. You need not worry that he will intrude into the body of the work which will be fast-moving (when it gets into the action sequences) and exceedingly detached. I introduce myself, in truth, only to remind you that these engines of creation are indeed powered by an individual no less idiosyncratic, difficult or painful to himself than you, although I have learned through tormenting years of apprenticeship ruthlessly to suppress all that is truly mine in the service of detached and transmuted work. (Even this use of "author" as character is a device, then; it is an invented persona which is in certain ways a metaphor for the real writer and in other ways not; it is a thing of spring and cheap bailing wire which, if it is handled correctly, will give you the impression that you know me when all you know is what I wish to present. So there.)

The author has been writing, with some success, for seven years now, but he was writing without success for a long time before that, and, therefore, his failure ratio, even taking into account his recent modest rise in reputation, is still convincing. Not only has the author always felt himself to be a young person, he has thought himself to be a young *failure;* but there is more strength in that because our youth and possibility may be stripped from us, but our failure can remain shining and constant forever. Sustained by his failure—to say nothing of a modest advance from his publisher—the author moves forward.

IV

Galaxies will be based heavily on two articles published in *Analog: Science Fiction & Fact* by the late John W. Campbell. Campbell for the last thirty-three years of his life (he died on 7/11/71) was the editor of that magazine under its present title and earlier identity, *Astounding Science Fiction*. He was a difficult man but not a dishonest one.

Campbell's articles put forth the existence of a "black" or lightless galaxy which would result from the implosion of a neutron star, the implosion unleashing terrible forces, causing a gravitational influence so strong as the star collapsed upon itself that the galaxy in which this occurred would trap not only light but space, and possibly time. A spaceship trapped within this black galaxy would be unable to get out. Escape velocity would, to counter gravity, have to exceed the implausible speed of light. All interstellar paths of flight would lead toward the gravitational field of this galaxy; none would lead away. Such a galaxy, Campbell pointed out, would be called Rome.

V

Neutron stars are white dwarves, inconceivably hot and dense, which burn furiously through their resources only to exhaust their fuel at a much earlier stage of their cycle of existence than so-called "normal" stars like our own humble Sol which, when its light is exhausted in several billion years, will probably decoalesce and disperse gently, therefore signaling the day of judgment, to say nothing of the rising of the dead and the sacred priests. Neutron stars cannot look forward to a long senility and a whimpering old age; they will depart to no nursing home of the heavens but instead are at a consistently *accelerating* combustion in order to maintain their existence, and when this acceleration reaches a point of no supply, matters do become rather cataclysmic. A day of judgment controlled by the life of a neutron star would be brief and would result, doubtless, in the recremation of the dead who, presumably, have already suffered enough.

VI

The novel to be based on this material would concern itself with a faster-than-light spaceship in the year 3902 which would tumble into the black galaxy and be unable to leave by tachyonic drive. ("Tachyonic" meaning *faster* than light, a device long beloved by science fiction writers, since we can keep our characters shuttling through the galaxies much as writers for the *Quarterly Review* can use subways and taxicabs for understandably slighter terrain, but a device useful here only if the ship can accelerate *up to* before moving beyond light speed.) Falling into the galaxy would be easy or at least inevitable, since one of the characteristics of the black galaxy is its invisibility, the implosive forces having contained light. Leaving, however, would be much more difficult. Leaving will be the concern of this novel.

Consider. Science fiction, since its formal inception as a romantic subgenre in this country in 1926 with the publication of the first issues of Hugo Gernsback's *Amazing Stories*, has best been known for its simple and melodramatic plots which demonstrate man's mastery (or later on, loss of control) of technology. The conventions of the genre then demand that the novel pivot upon the attempts of the crew to leave this entrapment and return to their planet of origin.

The ship is known—to us at least—as the *Skipstone*. It was completed in 3895 after a century-long effort of construction that involved the resources of many worlds and billions of the Systematized Forces. It is one of only fifteen faster-than-light ships now operating. Obviously something like this cannot be cheaply abandoned. The crew must return it to the fleet.

This problem-solving pivot is not one which I might attempt given my own devices. I am not a problem-solver by profession, let alone in my personal life. Left to myself I would be more interested in showing how the ship's inhabitants and cargo adjust to their new dwelling, how they set up light housekeeping in this unknown and difficult sector of the universe, but this would not do for the purposes of the science fiction novel. We must compete with, sell on the racks against *The Rammers of Arcturus*. It is important to understand, and I am sure that all of you do, that classically this field of science fiction was meant by its American originators to provide a road map from technological impasse, a map which would show us the way from a confusing and overpowering technology, to the wondrous society it could give us. Science fiction, then, is *technological fiction;* it is an attempt to relieve anxieties about the encroaching machinery by showing people how that machinery may be usefully applied. Science as benign instrumentation. *Amazing*'s earliest competitor was *Astounding Stories of Super-Science. Super-Science* brings us super-solutions. Thrilling Wonder. Astonishing Stories.

Details of the submission of *Skipstone*'s crew to the unknown should be dystopian. While the dystopian has an honorable tradition in science fiction, reaching earlier than *Amazing* to the works of Olaf Stapledon and H. G. Wells, it has really had a difficult time making its way, and even now, at a time of technological impasse and collapsed institutions, science fiction writers who go against the pro-technological format have a more difficult time in finding audiences and publishers than the traditionally oriented.

My own decision has been made, however: I would rather command an audience than not, to say nothing of publisher's advances, and therefore this construct, despite its bleaker aspects and a certain aura of cynicism which may occasionally drift off the pages, will be essentially cheerful, essentially hopeful, quite problem-solving and possessed of qualities of adventurousness. No writer of integrity with a wife and two helpless children could do less for the sake of his controlling artistic vision. This is to be kept in mind at all times.

VII

The Campbell articles were found by others and given to me; I did not locate them myself. There was a time in the late 1960s, early seventies, when I gave up altogether on *Analog*. Through no fault of my own (I felt), I was unable to read or relate to the contents of the magazine. Now I am back to reading it but not quite up to back issues. The articles were sent by people who thought I might be interested in basing a technologically oriented SF story on their contents. "Hard" science fiction they call it.

I have always had a certain awe for this kind of science fiction, and, although I cannot really do it well myself, wish that the genre had more of it. Unhappily "hard" science fiction is largely a myth; there is almost no science in science fiction and never has been. The recollected masterpieces of the 1940s were fantasies whose scientific basis was almost completely invented or could have been found in a general research work in five or ten minutes. At low word-rates, research is neither desirable nor profitable, since all markets pay the same for all stories that they publish, rewarding merit as they do the incompetent with a standard rate. Consequently, James Blish's science fiction writer is quoted as saying, "All the science I ever needed to know I got out of a bottle of scotch."

But how we could use it! Science, that is to say. We could indeed profit by technologically accurate science fiction. The awful expansion of our machinery, the technological manual as the poetics of the age, the rhythms of the machine as analogous to those of the newly discovered spirit . . . we need writers who can show us what the machines are doing to us in terms more systematized than those of random paranoia. A writer who could combine the techniques of modern fiction with a genuine command of science could be at the top of this field in no more than a few years. He would also stand alone.

There are a few among us who know science and a few more who understand fiction, but there is not a single science fiction writer who can do both. The one who has come closest, at least in his later work, is A—but A, although his undoubted gifts are the equal of any writer in America, is exhausted by a career of hackwork in his youth and embittered by the fact that his newer, important work has not distanced him from the hackwork but to most readers simply extends and reaffirms it. In any event A, like all science fiction writers, is invisible to the academic/literary nexus which controls judgments of literary reputation in America. He made wrong choices at the beginning. It is all his fault, of course, but one may nevertheless have sympathy for A.

B, a writer of equal technical range and even greater delicacy than A, also comes close to this ideal, but his science is weak and his output diminishing; he has, in any event, no interest in continuing to write science fiction and is making desperate attempts to leave the genre. Then there is C who has won a major literary award and is considered by many to be at the level of A or B, but C is clumsy and impenetrable and has little sense of compression. X, Y and Z have all in their way done interesting work but are burned out at the ages of, respectively, 2-, 2- and 2- and little can be expected of them. R had promise, of course, but has been dead for many years, and in terms of their literary contribution, O, P and T might just as well be, although one may wish them long life and health of days. Commercial writing is a difficult field for even its few successes. Ask A about this sometime.

Still, we deal not with A, B or the others (although they would make for an interesting study which I might someday do) but only with this writer, thirty-five years old and stricken M, easy to quick judgments of his contemporaries, slow to wrath or judgment of himself. I would like to accept that challenge: the welding of hard, technological insight with the full range of modern literary technique, but even so, a first confrontation with this material made me feel that I should pass it by. My personal life—I wanted to say this and in an earlier draft, in fact, did—my personal life is my black hole; my two daughters provide more correct and stiffening implosion than does any neutron star, and as far as the song of the pulsars, it is as nothing, as nothing at all to the sounds which come from the paddock area at Aqueduct Race Track in the Borough of Queens, New York, on a dark summer Tuesday. *Get me out, Angel; get that seven horse out flying.*

"No," I could have said like Cheever's adolescent in *Bullet Park*, "No, enough of your breathtaking concepts, infinite distances, quasar leaps, binding messages from the Crab Nebula; be away with your light years, asteroids, Van Allen belts, methane systems and heavy planets. No, I am aware that there are those who find an ultimate truth there and would bend their lives toward their perception but this is not for me. Where is the *pain*, the *remorse*, the *regret* and *guilt* and *terror*? No, I would rather dedicate the years of my productive life which remain to an understanding of the agonies of this middle-class suburb in northern New Jersey. Until I deal with those how can I comprehend Ridgefield Park, to say nothing of Scarsdale, Shaker Heights or the unknown lands of the west? Give me not the year two million which I will not see; give me now. The year two million can say nothing to me, but I may address it if, of course, the collected works can be carefully preserved. At least one writer will survive from this era and if not the notorious Q or the obscure N or the unfortunate A, why could it not be me?"

Nicely put. Cheever's adolescent would have approved, if not Cheever. Indeed, I found it convincing, until it occurred to me in one of those quick changes of consciousness which control the lives of all of us yet which may never be acknowledged in fiction that Ridgefield Park would forever be as mysterious to me as the swamp of lights perceived through the refinery smog which are known to my children as "stars" . . . and that one should never deny infinity to pursue a particular which until the day of one's death—if not for longer than that—would always be a mystery.

So I decided to try *Galaxies* after all, although with some trepidation. I felt better when I came to understand that it did not have to be a novel but merely a set of notes for one. Knowing this I was not shamed nor did I grieve, for one's life is merely a set of notes for a life and Ridgefield Park merely a rough working model of Trenton in which nonetheless several thousand people live unable to divine their right hand from their left, and also some cattle. Shalt thou have not pity on the cattle? For they too grew up and perished in a night.

VIII

So in the novel, which takes place in 3902, the spacecraft *Skip-stone*, on an exploratory flight through the major and minor galaxies surrounding the Milky Way, falls into the black galaxy of a neutron star and is lost forever.

The captain of *Skipstone* and the only living consciousness aboard is its woman commander, Lena Thomas. True now, all true: the hold of the ship carries five hundred and fifteen of the dead, sealed in their gelatinous fix, absorbing the unshielded ultraviolet of space which will at some future time hearken their reconstitution. True that yet another part of the enormous hold contains inactivated prostheses in which have been installed the personalities of seven skilled engineers who could be switched on at only slight inconvenience, who would provide Lena not only with answers to any problems technical but also with compan-ionship to while away the long and grave hours of this flight; true also that Lena's consciousness would, if it were so directed, reel and teem with memory, the rich and variegated colors of all the associations she has had through her twenty-eight years, aided by a whiff of psychogenics to augment the totality of her recall. True that, as has been explained to her during training, solitude is merely a state of mind and has little to do with the interior geography of the soul in which we all must reside.

True. All of it. Lena, however, does not use the prostheses until the time that *Skipstone* falls into the black galaxy nor has she had any desire to. She is a willful person, highly skilled and competent at least in relation to the routine tasks of this testing flight and quite self-reliant. To call upon artificial engineers for aid would be an admission of weakness, as would any resort to the dead who are, of course, dead and cannot be reached. She feels that to lean upon anything outside of herself would only be an admission of weakness, would be carried back to the Bureau by the monitors which constantly scan the ship to report gross physical functions and only the Bureau knows what else and this would lessen her chances for promotion at the end of the voyage. Lena is reasonably ambitious and propelled by self-interest; it is not unfair to her to say this or to point out that much of what occurs in her mind and actions from henceforth are spurred by selfish motives. In this sense her humanity is merely increased; witness is borne to it.

(In her suspicions she is quite right. The Bureau monitors everything. Not only are there biological readouts, but also visual scanners which transmit all activities aboard to tape at headquarters which when fed through another machine can reconstitute the interior of the ship. One can barely conceive the efficacy of the monitors to which Lena is exposed. Our own astronauts could have functioned under a sheath of independence so complete is the Bureau's fashioning of images. To be sure the monitoring ceases immediately as the ship falls into the black galaxy . . . but Lena is not sure of this and even then moderates her responses with caution. She has lived too long in *Skipstone* under the assumption that she has been spread out into a series of charts on a desk somewhere which reveal everything, even desires of which she is unaware.)

Sometimes Lena thinks that she would like to talk to the dead. Her feelings toward them are not as ruthless as those toward the Bureau or toward the prostheses; her condition, as she rattles in the hold of the ship moving on tachyonic drive, often seems to approximate theirs. Although they are deprived of consciousness, that quality seems almost irrelevant to the condition of hyperspace, and if there were any way in which she could bridge their mystery, she might well address them. What would she say to the dead? Anything, of course; just whatever comes into your mind, but she does not wish the Bureau to think she is mad. Surely they would adduce dialogues with the dead as evidence of insanity. So, caught between desire and necessity, she must settle for imaginary dialogues deep within the cells of consciousness and for long, quiescent periods when she will watch the monitors, watch the rainbow of hyperspace, witness the collisions of the spectrum. And say nothing whatsoever. Deny her life. It is a ship, at times, like this: utterly of the dead and yet beyond.

Lena, however, is not always mute. On certain occasions she will talk incessantly, as a matter of fact, if only to herself. (Her interior dialogue at these rare and explosive moments—when thoughts of the Bureau fall from her mind and she is only a lonely and frightened woman—is helpful, because in *Galaxies* dialogue will be important, both to heighten dramatic incident and to break up the long and inevitably difficult sections of expository prose.)

No device better than dialogue has been found to persuade the paperback reader, skimming a book on the newsstand, to opt for purchase. It gives a book a look of accessibility, gives the reader the assurance that he can penetrate it, and to say this is not to cast aspersion but to pay the reader the respect due his simple deductive insight. We must, all of us, become more human and can communicate our humanity only in the way that we deal with one another.

"Is that not so?" Lena asks the monitors, whispering in the darkness.

"Oh, it is surely so," she imagines that they say to her, "we become human only by approaching those who are of ourselves and by sharing our thoughts with them."

"Well then there is nothing wrong in talking to you."

"Not at all."

"I need to talk to you."

"You should. You certainly should."

"Who can make judgments that it is wrong to talk? Does Bureau know what is going on here?"

"Of course not."

"Do the dead? Do the engineers?"

"No. No again."

"Only I know."

"You and we, Lena, you and we."

"Of course. So I will continue to talk to you when I wish to do so."

"You should."

"I will."

"Thank you."

"Thank *you*."

Thus dialogue to open the partitions of the novel. It will play the same role here that repetitive sex scenes play in the pornographic novel. We cannot use sex here, since sex could hardly be conducted in *Skipstone*. With whom would she have it? Also the role of sex in science fiction is uncertain; it is an uneasy addition to a category of literature many of whose readers find sex (or at least written sex) directly uncomfortable.

Sex does not play an insignificant role in Lena's inner life, and eventually this issue will have to be discussed, in the best taste of course, but for now we consider merely the matter of dialogue. Lena talks to herself. She has dialogues with herself, with the monitors, often with the dead. She roams the ship and declaims. She maintains soliloquies, sometimes for hours. "Consider," she will for instance say to the dead this time, "consider what is going on here," the dead quiescent in the hold, some of them here for eight hundred years, others scaled down from that to only a few weeks, the recent dead and the far-gone dead nestled in the same gelatinous container that has been transferred wholly into the ship, "Consider where we are now," pointing through the hold, the colors gleaming through the portholes onto her wrist, colors dancing in the air, her eyes full and maddened in this light which is not to say that she *is* mad but that the condition of hyperspace is itself insane. The Michelson-Morley effect has a psychological as well as physical reality. "Why now," she says, "it could be *me* dead and in the hold and all of you here in the dock watching the colors spin, all the same, living and the dead together as we move faster than light," she says . . . and indeed she is right. The tachyonic drive has such a profound effect upon subjective reality that the living can become the dead, the dead the living.

Faster-than-light speed drives all things toward the center of the Bell Curve of existence, you see. Here the dead live, the living are dead, all together in that mix as she has pointed out, and were it not that the objective poles of her consciousness remain fixed intensely by her years of trained discipline, she would press the levers, eject one by one the dead into the larger coffin of space, something which is indicated only as an emergency procedure under the gravest of circumstances and which would result in her removal from command post immediately upon her return. It would be an outrageous action, for the dead are precious cargo: their accumulated estates, willed toward preservation and revival, have, in essence, funded the faster-than-light experiments.

"I will handle you with the greatest delicacy," Lena says. "I will treat you with great respect and I will never, oh, I will never let you go, little packages in your little prisons, exquisite goods, delightful cargo, precious weight," and so on and on as the *Skipstone* moves in excess of one hundred and eighty-six thousand miles per second. Indeed it now moves at two point three million miles per second, still accelerating . . . and yet except for the colors, the nausea, the disorienting swing, her own mounting insanity, the terms of this novel as it must be written, were it not for all of this, Lena might be in the IRT Lenox Avenue local at rush hour moving slowly uptown as circles of illness track her in the fainting car in the bowels of summer in New York in 1975 as mortality, known over and again, presses in.

IX

But the novel is not of mortality but immortality. It is of the vaulting extension of human life as it will be known not only within the spaces of the ship, but also in the minds that one by one, painfully in that hold, are being freed by radiation to tenant the cyborgs that have been constructed precisely against such an emergency. Of the dead, Lena will learn much more. Of herself she knows much already. As *Galaxies* opens she is twenty-eight years old.

It is almost two thousand years in the future. Man has established colonies on forty planets in the Milky Way, including the system of Sirius, the well-known Dog Star; he has fully populated the solar system, except for Jupiter whose methane gases are not only inimical to life, but also destructive to the gearing of life support. Jupiter, thus, was given up for lost in 2814, but all of the other planets are populated and on several of them—Venus, Neptune, Titan, largest moon of Saturn notably—there is already severe evidence of overpopulation and the breakdown of social and technological systems. For this reason great emphasis has been placed upon the faster-than-light experiments which will, hopefully, open up worlds outside the few already known that might not be inimical to human life. The three planets of Sirius already have a fragile colony, the Antares Cluster has twenty worlds upon which autonomous colonists are presumed to exist, but this is not sufficient, and now the social engineers and philosophers of this time, who are no more numerous or farsighted than those of our present, predict the collapse of the multitechnological system within a century unless more space is found.

The colonies of the solar system are under the government of Earth, and on Earth a feudal system has been reconstituted, an autocracy with nobles, vassals and a hereditary monarchy. But fortunately none of these need be developed in the novel. They will merely lurk in the background, a set of assumptions underlying, perhaps, Lena's character or the necessity of certain confrontations, but not developed. It will be understood, of course, that the alienation produced by a feudal/hierarchical system works upon almost all those not high in the hierarchy and that Lena's anguish is social as well as metaphysical.

It is 3902. Still, the medical science of that distant time is not notably superior to that of our own in terms of human mortality. The life-span has not been significantly extended, and although certain serious illnesses have been almost erad-icated—heart seizure by cortisone derivatives in the late twen-tieth century, cancer through horse antibodies in the middle 2500s, cerebrovascular accident by glandular therapy only two hundred years ago—others have risen to take their place as if certain universal laws of mortality must be served, diseases only being their humble agents. So nephritis is killing people now, and arteriosclerosis and pancreatitis are major killers. Menin-gitis, transmuted into a hereditary disease, is a common cause of mortality over eighty. All in all the life-span is only five or ten years longer than what it is during our time, say seventy-seven years for men, eighty-four or eighty-five for women. Perhaps this is tragic, but perhaps it is not; there is no way that humanity would ever have been able to deal with the social chaos produced by a greatly extended life-span or practical immortality; the systems in which men have always lived are geared to common mortality tables as are the institutions.

Indeed, most of the dead embalmed in the hold were merely in their sixties or seventies. There is irrelevant irony in the fact that man can have at least established peripheral colonies through sections of the Milky Way, can travel through most of it, can have solved the mysteries of the FTL drive and constructed such a craft as *Skipstone* and yet finds his own biology as stupefying and mysterious as he did in Elizabethan times. But, then, every sociologist understands that those who live in a culture are least qualified to judge it, because they have so fully assimilated the codes of the culture that they are unable to be objective, and Lena does not see this irony any more than it is necessary for the reader to in order to appreciate the deeper and more metaphysical irony of *Galaxies*. Which is this:

That greater speed, greater space, greater progress, greater sensation has not resulted in any real expansion of the limits of consciousness and personality . . . and that Lena, much less than appreciating the wonders of the FTL drive, merely perceives it as a form of further entrapment and delimitation.

(This is a familiar theme in my work: that the expansion of technology will only delimit consciousness, create greater feelings of alienation, impotence, hopelessness and so on, and that the neurological/psychological equipment of our species is programmed to record sensations equally alien in the stars or on the sea. Although many literary critics and philosophers tend toward this vision, most science fiction readers or writers do not, since science fiction is about control, not dysfunction. Still, I beg your various indulgences, pointing out that, even if matters are not hopeless, writing *about* hopelessness may serve cautionary ends just as the sermons of John Calvin enabled Puritans of the seventeenth century to better appreciate their lot on Earth. I am doing the best I can, just as each of you is doing the best you can, and I am as much in awe of *Skipstone* as is Lena; in fact my awe is greater than hers, since *Skipstone* is my creation.)

X

Lena is merely a technician. Let us not misunderstand this; it is crucial. Although she is highly skilled and has been trained by Bureau personnel for many years, she really does not need to possess much more than the knowledge of any graduate physicist of her time. Her role, which is essentially to maintain the ship on its preselected course and respond to computer check-out, could be done by any of our own astronauts, could, in fact, be done by anyone capable of flying a single-engine plane. The nature of the investment, however, has demanded that Lena be intellectually qualified far beyond the true demands of her job, and this leads to boredom, depression and further alienation, the Bureau not understanding in the fortieth century what NASA does not understand now: there is no one happier than he or she who is in a position utilizing fullest capacity, no one more prone to depression and incompetence than the overqualified.

Lena is doing it for the money, to be sure. It is the only rational motive with which she can live. Certainly she is not an idealist. No idealist would study for a decade in order to take on cargo of the dead.

When she is finished with this latest probe, three months hence, she has decided that she will return to her quarters on Uranus and request a six-month leave. She is entitled to it, and surely the Bureau will not object; after her debriefing is concluded, it cannot hold her. She will not be denied and she will insist upon the leave. She is only twenty-eight, as young or a little younger in her culture than she would be in ours, and she does not like having been sent with the dead to tumble through the spectrum of the tachyons for weeks at a time. She would like to be, at least for a while now, a young woman. She would like to be at peace. She would like to be taken for herself and not merely as a lever of FTL manipulation. She would not mind being loved. She would not mind a physical relationship. Her needs are the needs of any of you.

XI

Saying that Lena "would not mind a physical relationship," which is a delicate way of saying for the category market that she would enjoy some sex, means that we must confront the element of sex in this novel if only because it deals with a female protagonist. Culture is culture, Ti-Grace to the contrary, and readers would not stand for the idea of asepsis with a young woman, although they would not be similarly suspicious if Lena were an attractive young man. Still, this is *modern, literary* science fiction where some credence is given to the entire inferred range of human needs and desires. One cannot ignore the issue of the sexuality of the protagonist.

And the easy scenes could be included and to stunning literary effect; perhaps in the final draft they might be. The writer could win high marks for his poetic vision if not his subtlety. Lena masturbating as she stares through the porthole at the colored levels of hyperspace, that space a series of steps that seem to lead her, twitch by twitch upon the lever of the clitoris to the very altar of self. Lena dreaming thickly of intercourse, as deep in sleep she massages her nipples, the ship plunging deeper this instant (as she could not possibly know) toward the black galaxy, the black galaxy itself some sort of ultimate vaginal symbol whose Freudian overcast would not be ignored in the imagery of the novel as it has been ignored in the imagery of little modern science fiction. Indeed one can envision Lena stumbling toward the evictors at the depths of her panic in the black galaxy as she tries to bring out one of the dead, struggling with it in the blocks, her grim and necrophiliac fantasies as the body moves slowly on its glistening slab, the way her eyes would look as she slowly comes to the awareness that, through the devices of autoeroticism, she has become one of the dead, indistinguishable from the body that is risen . . . oh, this could be a powerful scene indeed; almost anything having to do with sex in space is powerful, and one must conjure also with the possible effects of hyperspace upon the orgasm. I would face the issue unintimidated and in line with the use to which the novel can place powerful and effective dialogue.

Dialogue:

"For God's sake," Lena would say at the end, the music of her entrapment squeezing, coming over her, rending her toward extinction, "for God's sake, all that we ever sought was sex, that was what must have sent us into the tiers of space as well, that was all space ever meant to us, another level of extension. I've got to have it, do you understand?"

"Oh, yes," her partner, perhaps the dead itself would say, "I agree with you; you've got to have it."

"Then give it to me!"

"Oh, I will," her partner would say thoughtfully, "I will give it to you, but then think of sex being the life-force and representing so many other things. Are you *sure* you want it? You had better think this through very carefully."

"You're mad," she says, "you are mad; I'm pleading for you."

"But what are you pleading for?" her partner says, moving slowly; "unless you know, I'm afraid that I had better not cooperate; I wouldn't want to give you what you think you're seeking only for you to learn that all of this was a lie; we can't be lied to; we have got to face the truth now," lying across her, odors coming in little whiffs from his body, which is, of course, utterly corrupt, the cryonic factor being lock to death rather than its obliteration. "I'd like to do it very much you understand; I agree with you that this may be the only freedom that we can find—"

"Must you talk?"

"But of course! Inexhaustibly. It may be our only freedom, but I can't quite give it to you. I can't give you what you want. I'm not quite right you see," he would point out, his wasted little limbs like the wings of a ruined bird's fluttering upon her. "Terribly sorry."

"*Sorry?*"

"Yes, surely, but after all you are demanding more than you can possibly be given. You are—"

"No," she would say, "no, I don't want to hear your excuses, don't want to hear any of that at all. It does no good, it excuses nothing, get inside me, get inside me, damn it! Don't you understand this is the only thing we ever wanted?" seizing his wasted organs, dropping them with disgust as she sees them like a pendulum hung within her hand, giving up then and pushing him away with revulsion to jam her fingers instead through her aqueous surfaces, slippery and waiting, opening up the walls to the image of a culmination that if she could only touch she could have then, swimming through the surfaces of the self, but the nearer she gets to it the further seems the climax, and not only that but there is something else wrong, something nagging at the periphery of realization, if she could only touch it—

Well, if she could touch it, then she would, but this is not the direction that the novel would take, at least in the present conceptualization. Attempts at poetry fall into the pornographic tumble, one variety of pulp becomes another, organs are substituted for machinery and the center takes hold of all. Say it and be done then: space *is* asepsis; it cancels differences, renders sexuality barren. That has been the secret of the power of science fiction for almost fifty years. It is not deceit or its adolescent audience or publication codes or difficult editors which have deprived our literature of the range of human sexuality, but the fact that in the clean and abysmal spaces between the stars, sex, that demonstration of our perverse and irreplaceable humanity, would have no role at all. For we are not human out there in any way which can join with another; our humanity, frail at best, is fully concentrated within ourselves to defend ourselves against the void.

Consider. It was not casual that our astronauts returned to give us their vision of otherworldliness, not casual that they staggered in their thick landing gear as they came under the salute on board, not casual that White screamed on his space walk and begged to return to the capsule or Carpenter shouted *get me out of here!* Not for nothing did all of those marriages, all of those wonderful kids undergo such terrible strains as many went undersea or toward poetry, hypnosis, transcendental meditation. Sex was squeezed out of them up there and many have not yet recovered. It does not fit. It will never occupy any meaningful role in all of the history of space travel.

Lena knows this. Somewhere toward the end of the novel she would in fact come to terms. "I never thought of sex," she would say, "never thought of it once, not even at the very end when everything was exploding around and I was falling."

XII

Naturally when we speak of the absence of sex at this time we are dealing only with the faster-than-light craft and their solitary voyagers; the conventional ferry ships, those that take people at sublight speeds from planet to planet, from star to star within the galaxies, are populated by the ordinary voyagers of their time and like ordinary voyagers of any time; they couple randomly or otherwise, stare through the portholes and think of their wasted lives, perform their hasty scuttling in the dark. In all cultures at any stage of their history, sex will be important, but it does not seem to have anything to do with the opening of new frontiers, which is, of course, Lena's mission and which will similarly be the mission of this novel.

XIII

Thirty-nine zero two. There has yet been no contact with intelligent extraterrestrial life, although humanity has colonized many planets and investigated several thousand more. This seeming exclusivity of human intelligence baffles cosmologists and mathematicians while pleasing the theologians; perhaps humanity is unique in the universe, perhaps by the laws of chance it is to be expected that, in nearly two thousand years of exploration, contact with an intelligence other than our own in a limitless universe would be highly unlikely. Bovine animals found on a planet of Sirius have turned out to have an intelligence close to that of birds and are the most intelligent race yet encountered, but these animals—called Sirians by the uninventive colonists—have enough xenophobia to be dying off slowly, their grazing culture succumbing to fires which the colonists have set for the purposes of atmospheric balance. It would be nice to compound the myth of faster-than-light drive with deeper and richer myths of strange races amidst the great stars, but this cannot be.

The farther humanity voyages, then, the more it seems merely to confront itself. At least this is the point of view which

Galaxies will take. This is merely one of a set of alternatives. One could write colorful chapters about the many strange, civilized races colonists have encountered, all of them celebrative of man and his works, except for those few misguided who would fight him and so would have to be destroyed. That would be polemic, however. Despite the excesses of my youth, polemic has no place even in a science fiction novel. Leave those innocent races alone. Upon investigation they would be found out to be not so damned innocent at all. Too, the higher the level of innocence, the more room there is for corruption.

XIV

Because of the asepsis and the fact that she is alone on the ship when the novel opens and there are no intelligent aliens, it will be necessary to obtain characterization for Lena, definable idiosyncrasy, in some other fashion. Some channel, then, will have to be found to trigger conflict and color and that opportunity will come only through the moment of crisis, that moment at which *Skipstone* is drawn slowly into the black galaxy of the neutron star.

Now this moment will occur fairly early into the novel. Perhaps only eight or nine thousand words of expository material will precede the disaster. There will be a shade of exposition in which the spectra of hyperspace are interwoven with Lena's fantasy and then, her only indication a quiver in the gut of the ship, *Skipstone* will fall. It will fall for twenty-five billion miles with its load of the dead and its screaming pilot. It will fall not only through space, but also through time, but of time Lena will know nothing at all, only of her pain and her astonishment.

To explain why she screams during the fall, it is important to explain hyperspace. To Lena the tachyonic drive is merely to draw the curtains across the portholes and to be in a cubicle.

There is no cessation of motion in hyperspace; there could not possibly be, the drive taking the ship past any concept of light or motion and into an area where there is no language to encompass nor glands to register. Were Lena to draw these curtains (similar in their frills and pastels to what at one time hung in the author's own familial home), she would be deprived of any sensation; but of course she cannot; she must open them to the portholes and through them she can then see the song of the colors.

Inside, in tachyonic drive, there is for Lena a deep and painful wretchedness, a feeling of terrible loss not unlike the emotions of the unknowing and invisible dead which may be ascribed to the effects of hyperspace upon the psyche. But these sensations can be shielded. They are not visible from the outside and can be completely controlled by the phlegmatic personalities who comprise most of the pilots of these interstellar flights. Lena herself is phlegmatic. She reacts more to stress than do some of her counterparts, but she is well within the normal range prescribed by the Bureau, which, it must be admitted, tends to do a rather superficial job of profiling.

But phlegmatic or not, contained or not, the effects of falling into the black galaxy are entirely different from the hyperspace in which *Skipstone* "normally" dwells, and it is here where Lena's emotional equipment comes apart.

XV

And it is here where the *writer's* emotional equipment begins to come apart as well; the writer, no mere engine of creation, has his own problems with which to deal. His powers fail, likewise his will, his desire, a welter of personal difficulties which are rightfully no concern of the reader (do not worry about them) similarly overwhelm. He is exploited by a series of weaknesses which his own novels savagely probe and exploit the way that a surgeon's cunning tool might burst rather than remove a cyst. The writer's background in physics is slight, his astronomy shaky, his astronautics shakier yet nor does he grasp chemistry. He has a certain feeling for the scientific spirit, but surely this cannot carry him through. What he lacks is that systematized and rigorous grasp of the hard sciences which the novel will have to utilize in order to succeed, and the writer cannot rely, at least this one time, upon his stylistic gifts to carry him through.

The writer's stylistic gifts are notable. Even he will testify to that. For many years he has been able to write in the style and vision of almost any writer living or preferably dead: he is a skillful parodist, a creator of pastiche so smooth as to be almost undetectable from the original. He has access to rhetorical tricks and devices which have time and again enabled him to force his way through a difficult novel on technique alone. From publisher to publisher the writer has carried his little carnival with its cheap masks, greasepaint, assortment of mirrors and depressed freaks; even when the spirit has failed him yea unto the very sinuses, his magic and revolving light shows, with the energetic cooperation of his freaks, never have. But for reasons which the writer cannot quite understand—is it possible that he has been smitten by artistic integrity?—he does not want magic and revolving freak and light show inc. to perform its wondrous if somewhat mechanical convolutions this time. He would like to do this novel the difficult way, which is to say upon the basis of its rather awesome and terrible concept, but he does not know if he has the courage, he does not know if he can summon the will to work on his research base or even to command the material. He is not sure, like Lena herself, that he belongs in a project of this sort at all, and therefore only with much moaning and groaning does he address himself to the task which this one time he will not write himself out of but into . . . and courage, he has decided, has nothing to do with this at all. Ignore everything above. Courage is facing a man with a gun or protecting your wife against attack or risking your job to protest policies you despise or running a mile in three fifty-seven flat when the heart seems turned to ashes. Nothing to do with the writing of fiction, particularly science fiction, has anything to do with courage. Do not let anyone tell you otherwise. Most science fiction writers are drunks and almost all of them have unhappy lives. A, B and C.

XVI

The *Skipstone* falls into the black galaxy. Needed here are great gobs of physics; astronautic and mathematical data must likewise be transmitted. If they are not, *Galaxies* would be a space romance, a work of fantasy, and this is no fantasy at all. The heavy-science data must be furnished in a way, however, which will illuminate the reader without repelling him.

In traditional literature this is not so easy; in science fiction it never is quite so difficult. A science fiction writer does not have to worry as much as a literary writer about impelling his audience by trying to teach it. Readers of this genre *expect* to be bored; in fact they are seeking boredom as a means of release from too much self-confrontation. They *want* bad writing as well, because bad writing does not energize; it makes almost no one (except stuffy critics and jealous fellow writers) uncomfortable. Science fiction readers, thus, will sit for a lecture much more willingly than would, say, the sophisticated readers of the esteemed John Cheever who could hardly bear sociological diatribes spliced into those already difficult landscapes. Thus it would be possible without awkwardness or the need to dramatize to put down a hard body of facts, and these facts could indeed be set off from the novel. They would be a separate chapter.

Through all of the time that these facts are being articulated, Lena is in the black galaxy, stunned and suffering, and this is certainly too bad for her, but life is cruel, art is everlasting, one must treat characters cruelly in order to make a point. They are, after all, constructions; they have no existence. A writer with compassion for his characters is a writer without guile or control, uninterested in the truth. Fictional characters must be manipulated coldly; they permit this, having no choice. Would that this were true for all characters and not those merely confined to the contract between writer and reader.

XVII

In some of the myriad galaxies which revolve through the known portion of the universe, a universe which is either finite, expanding or circular (the debate continues in 3902; perceptions of the size of the universe have expanded through the millennia, but there are those who say that a limit has been found), there exist phenomena known as neutron stars.

Neutron stars, several hundred times the size of "average" stars such as Sol or Sirius, must, because of their gigantic dimension, create and consume energy at a fearsome rate of atomic combustion merely to sustain themselves. In this sense, neutron stars, like all heavenly constructions, are sentient: they fight for self-preservation in the way that our near planets fight for life by spinning faster than those distant; if they did not do so, they would fall into the Sun and be consumed. So does the neutron star ferociously consume its energy.

But as the energy is being eaten away by the violence of combustion, so it must run out, and for this reason the neutron star will collapse in a mere ten to fifteen thousand years as opposed to the hundreds of millions which a "normal" star will have . . . and as that neutron star reaches the end of its cycle, its hydrogen fuses to helium, then nitrogen and even heavier elements, the atoms grabbing stray electrons in a frantic attempt to maintain atomic reaction, and then with an implosion of cosmic force, all power gone, the neutron star collapses upon itself.

All is disaster.

Ah, the lamentations of Jeremiah! It is not merely that the dying neutron stars destroy themselves, collapsing inward at the speed of light, layers of gases crowding, grappling with one another, falling into that diminished core . . . that is a pretty enough sight in itself—we may see it in our spectroscopes and telescopes as the nova—but this is merely the beginning of what the neutron star, ending, can do. For it can destroy the galaxy by which it was enveloped.

The gravitational force created by this implosion would be so vast as to literally seal in light. Small planets have slight gravity, larger objects heavier; the gravity on Jupiter greatly exceeds that of our Earth . . . but how much greater than Jupiter's is Sol's, how much greater than Sol's the gravity of massive Antares into which almost all of our solar system in its orbit would fit? And the neutron star, which could contain five or ten thousand Antares before its collapse, could create a gravity which would overcome all speeds presently understood. Light travels at a hundred and eighty-six thousand miles per second. That might not be sufficient to escape from the ruined core.

And not only light. Sound, heat, the properties of all the stars would be sucked into that great tube of force. The galaxy itself might be drawn into the funnel of gravitation created by the collapse and be absorbed slowly into the flickering and desperate heart of the extinguished star.

XVIII

Most of this theory would be news to Lena, of course. Even two thousand years in the future. She is not a theorist but a technician, and as the *Skipstone* begins its descent into the black galaxy, all that she would know would be pain, but it would be pain of such dimension that she would not have the language for it, a pain so profound that it might be interpreted as pleasure or as any one of a hundred other things. Tumbling, tumbling, as the animal in the center claws for her.

XIX

The existence of neutron stars and their disastrous outcome would make several extrapolations reasonable. Of the existence of these stars there is no doubt; they are being dealt with (along with ruined celebrities and the politics of Mozambique and the political fallout of the radical middle) in our most prominent Sunday supplements. The articles on which the astronomic theory of *Galaxies* is in part based are in themselves based upon a body of theory which has been widely accepted as a result of the researches of the last decade.

Just a few extrapolations follow:

One: The gravitational forces created by the implosion would, like great spokes wheeling from the star, drag in all sections of the galaxy within their compass, and because of the force of that gravitation, the galaxy would be invisible. Gravitation would contain light. Hit a certain section of space as has *Skipstone* where nothing has been mapped and find a galaxy. Galaxies themselves, of course, are merely interruptions in the lightless canvas of the universe.

Two: The neutron star, functioning as a cosmic vacuum cleaner (all right, this is homey imagery but then good science fiction should make the mysterious, the terrible, the inviolable as comfortable and accessible as one's own possessions, just as pornography should make the fires of sex little more than a twitch, easily untwitched, in the familiarly tumescent genitalia), might literally destroy the universe. *The entire universe.* Indeed, the universe may be in the process at this moment of being broken down as hundreds of millions of its planets and their suns are being inexorably drawn in the mesh of their galaxies toward the great vortices of the neutron stars. It would be a slow process, to be sure; here one is talking about many billions of years . . . but one is also talking about a span of time that may someday be measured in finite terms and which thus gives inexorable cast to all human endeavor.

("Hey, Joe, look at this! The print-out says that in two billion, three hundred and fifty-two million years and change the universe is going to be destroyed!"

("Let me look at that, Tom. Hey, this is frightening! This is terrible news but it all seems to check out."

("We'd better tell the President. We'd better go right in there now and tell him."

("No. Wait."

("What?"

("I said wait, Tom. I do not know if they can handle information like this at the present time."

("It is our obligation."

("Our obligation to what? Make science a mere servant of the state? No . . . we must conform to a higher ethic."

("Only two billion, three hundred and fifty-two million to go. I don't know what to say. Only that . . . only that we'll miss it all terribly.")

A single neutron star, at least theoretically, could absorb the universe given limitless time and of that there would be nothing in the universe as we know it. There are quite a few neutron stars.

Three: But, then, the universe may have, looking at it the other way, been *created by* such an implosion, that implosion throwing out enormous cosmic filaments, which in flickering instants of time which are as eons to us but mere instants to the cosmologists, are now being drawn in like a child's paddle ball extended on a rubber string, now falling back. Those filaments lead to the neutron star. The galaxies may be a by-product of the implosion; existence as we know it may be an accidental offshoot, an interruption in the cycle controlled by the neutron star whose creation and expulsion are the true ordering force of the universe.

This would either cancel vanity or make it stronger.

Four: Consider this astronautically for a moment, ignoring questions of cosmology. A ship trapped in such a vortex, such a black or invisible galaxy, drawn toward the deadly source of the neutron star, would be unable to leave through normal faster-than-light drive; because the gravitation would absorb light it would be impossible to build up through acceleration to escape velocity. (Accelerative velocities are sub-faster-than-light.) If it were then possible to emerge from the field, it could be done so only by an immediate switch to the tachyonic drive without acceleration. This is a process which could well drive the occupants of the ship insane and which would, in any case, give no clear destination. At the point of breakout the flight would be uncontrollable. The black hole of the dead star is a literal vacuum in space. One could fall through the hole but where, then, where would one go?

And when? To what time?

Five: The mere process of *falling* toward the dead star would be a state incomprehensible to current understanding of biophysics or chronology. It would certainly make one insane.

XX

So one can understand now why Lena would not know that *Skipstone* had fallen into the black galaxy until, with no sense of transition, she would simply be there. Not that anticipation would have done her much good. There is literally no way to plan for events like this. One cannot create vectors for madness.

XXI

These fragments of technological data having been stated, the crisis of the novel—the fall into the black galaxy—having already occurred, it would be necessary in terms of a smoothly plotted story line with a rising level of excitement to describe then the actual sensations incurred by *Skipstone*'s entrapment in the field of the neutron star.

This is not unreasonable. Science fiction, after all, is all that most of us will ever be able to know of the technological wonders of the future, and although it is true that the majority of us are not *interested* in the future, having more than we can handle, mostly, in coming to terms with the unspeakable present, there is a small and dedicated group of readers to whom the future has at least as much meaning as their circumstances and these, the science fiction audience for the most part, should not be disappointed. One would not want to skimp on the details. Even at its relatively low word rates (and this must be understood, they are quite low in relation to the amount of invention needed and time expended), science fiction in the hands of its best writers has always been a generous medium, offering more detail than would strictly speaking be necessary from the standpoint of mere plotting, of simple manipulation of characters through obstacles. Indeed, science fiction often suffers from the weakness of too much background, too little foreground, skimping of characterization in favor of unassimilated futurological details, but at this point the construct hints at breaking down into a series of grumbling little essays about the state of the art and this is not the author's intention.

I will resist this. Polemic, after all, is not fiction nor does fiction serve didactic purposes and remain art, and the author's opinions, artistic or polemical alike, are worthless; only his ability to transmute them through the material matters, and this is the contract with the reader. He will not be led away from *Skipstone* (not far, anyhow), the author will stay with the point, the novel will be science fiction and not merely *about* science fiction, and if the reader will stay around, I promise a smooth and satisfying read containing effortless little blocks of scientific data which will be of personal use. A little hard fact is by no evidence dangerous; it may be the last legitimate refuge of those of us who would still espouse—as does your suffering, tormented, lecherous and self-pitying author—the colorful tenets of Calvinism.

I would use, then, a surrealistic mode to describe Lena's descent into the galaxy. Conceive of what is happening now as *Skipstone* is gathered to that palm and crushed like sand downward: she sees, perhaps, grotesques slithering in dimensions on the walls, monsters that are really little recoveries of her past, plastered there in descent. Watching them whirl in pattern, scuttle on the bulkheads, she could reenact her life in full consciousness from birth to death, the grotesques merely being triggering projections of events from her history. She could indeed be turned inside out anatomically; she could perform in her imagination or in the flesh gross physical acts upon herself; she could live or die a thousand times in the lightless, timeless expanse of the pit . . . all of this could be done within the confines of this one section, the descent toward the neutron star. It would lead to some powerful insights if only properly handled.

One could do it in many ways. Picaresque would be a possibility, an episodic framework one should say, one perversity or lunacy to a chapter, the chapters interwoven with flatter, more expository sections on the gravitational effects, the biochemistry of descent, the physics of the force field. For instance, there might be a point at which Lena could take herself to be back in training, preparing for the ordeal of *Skipstone.*

In only a little while, she thinks, she will be responsible for the great ship and for its cargo of the dead, but now, staggering from the tube of the simulator, her vision is somewhat more limited. She sees the man who is responsible for her training, a man whom we will call John. Slightly disoriented, nauseated from the experiments, she finds herself speaking to him in a way that she has never before. "Why the dead?" she says. She moves her hands across the slate of cheekbones, whoops with little convulsions of nausea. "Why must we carry the dead?"

"There are many reasons."

"Tell me. Tell me one. Why must I take death into the stars when the stars were to bring us life?"

"Because it is they who have paid for much of this," John says, holding her tentatively. He is a wise and embittered man who believes that it is necessary for him to see and tell the truth at all times, and for these reasons he lives in great pain because his is not a truthful culture. "Without the moneys that are paid from the great trusts of the dead to make possible this first stage of their revival, they would be unable to finance the probes."

"It's not right."

"The conditions are stringent. The ultraviolet will restore them, with other things, to life someday. It is fortunate that their needs and ours have so meshed."

"But it is not right," Lena says, "it's not right; the dead are the dead and should not be tied to life. And what happens if something goes wrong in space? Am I responsible for all of them, then? What will become of me?"

"Waivers," John says. "There are careful and complete waivers which are signed, Lena; you can be sure of that. All will be taken care of."

He takes her, then, from the simulating crate, trying to ease her toward calm with many little pats and touches on her back, but Lena moves from him and says, "I don't want to travel with the dead. I can't bear it to feel that they're all in there with me."

"They have no consciousness."

"They're still *dead.*" Old fears and revulsions—the word is atavism, I suppose—persist.

'They are merely cargo."

"Cargo is cargo but these were people once."

"Lena, the costs of this are more enormous than anyone can grasp. The dead at least subsidize a little part of it, make it that much easier. Is it their fault that this is for them another opportunity to live again someday? Lena, we will all be dead someday. Are you prepared to say what you will do?"

She shakes her head. "I'm not going to be dead for a long time," she says, "but if I were to die now, I would accept it; I would not take down the living."

"How do you know?"

"I *know,*" she says, "I know what I am, what I would do; you have no right to say that I don't," and she then goes on to explain to John in a lucid fashion that makes a good deal of sense why this is so: why she cannot bear the presence of the dead on what she takes to be (she believes this if only to sustain her own mood) a mission that is life-seeking, but as she tries to explain this in a level, reasonable tone to John, something opens darkly within her, restraint vanishes and she is weeping convulsively against him.

John makes brusque, useless little gestures across her arms and shoulders, hoping that he will not break down himself and cry with her and for the *Skipstone*, for the dead in space. If he were to do this, he knows, he would never stop, that single lunge of feeling would take him all the way over the precipice of detachment and he would be gone forever; no good for Lena either; he must take care of her and so he gets hold of himself, swaddling Lena against him, leading her away from there under the confused gaze of other, less senior technicians who cannot possibly imagine the meaning of this scene but know that something has happened to their pilot and to their supervisor which will change the course of all preparations. Except that in this world nothing changes.

XXII

No, the technicians are wrong again; anyone who functions under the supposition of change surrounding these experiments would be wrong. The schedule for the mission is as rigorous and controlled as any of our own countdowns. So diabolically cunning are those in this Bureau of 3902 that they have even programmed into the countdown emotional breakdowns of the minor sort which Lena has just experienced, which has so unsettled John. (They have worked up the psychometrics; they know there will be no major breakdowns.) Not only the engineering but personalities have been taken into account by the cunning and nearly omniscient Bureau so that, while Lena and John feel that they have undergone a series of reactions, they are merely enacting what the psychologists had long since forecast as a momentary stress-tremor. Nothing that they have done since the beginning of training, not even the hasty and uncertain intercourse which they now undertake in the sterile cell of Lena's quarters, is not charted by the Bureau.

Of course Lena would like to feel that it is. If she were to know that her sudden coupling with John was part of her program and that the Bureau has calculated it almost to the minute of entrance, if John were to know that he occupies his position as training superior only because he has been judged most likely to give Lena a satisfactory sexual recollection to hold to herself in the void, both of them would be overcome with revulsion and their plotted coupling would not have taken place. They would have sprung from one another.

For these reasons the Bureau tries to make its involvement in the lives of its principals as subtle as possible, although every now and then, particularly in the matter of monitoring— on which it is adamant—its true impulse to control can be glimpsed. Still, who can blame it? From the vantage point of 1975, none of us can comprehend the forces which made it this way. The future of humanity, or so their computers and technicians hold, is dependent on the outcome of these FTL experiments. Unless the tachyonic drive can be used by the hundreds of thousands sent routinely voyaging to colonize, unless the space of *Skipstone* can someday, much enlarged, shield inexperienced travelers from the horrors of hyperdrive, humanity will remain confined to its precarious hold only upon portions of the Milky Way. The tachyons must work. The flight must be accomplished. The investment in *Skipstone* and in Lena is absolute.

So who is to begrudge these two or the Bureau their desperate moments of communion in her quarters? Not now; not these two. Certainly not the author who here would bring out his rhetorical arsenal to prove that sex in the future is very much the same as sex in the present or past. (This kind of approach is very reassuring to readers of science fiction, to say nothing of the author himself who has the feeling that he has been missing something most of his life.) And then, too, the author has a wicked hand with a sex scene, always did, is a master of the pornographic literary or the literary pornographic, depending upon your point of view.

"Oh, my God, you must do it to me," Lena would shriek, a little floridly, but floridity under stress is one of her more charming habits; she becomes more rather than less dignified when excited and indulges in archaisms of speech. "You must do it to me quickly, you must do it to me now, you must penetrate me swiftly to the core and make me close upon you in the arc of my need," her nipples bursting like little flowers, or, more in tune with the material, one might say that they are the dull purple of methane. "I want it now, I really do want it now, John; you have got to give it to me, for I cannot, truly cannot stand it anymore," and John, grunting not only with need but with a reluctance which he has always felt with her, finds her desirable, yet there is something within her that he cannot touch, something which he thinks of as eternally *measuring*, moves toward the task, poised on his knees, running his hands over the slab of her body, his flesh seeming to retract as nevertheless he covers the pilot of *Skipstone* and begins to move upon her slowly, unrhythmically, pausing now and then to wipe his streaming brow with a veined, competent supervisor's hand. Silent during sex—the clinical opposite of Lena, he finds himself speechless during the act, performing it in a reverent manner—he nevertheless conducts an interior monologue. I don't know why I'm doing this, he thinks; I can't imagine what the point of this is; it isn't having her for the meaning of the act but only to satisfy something within her, and he comes close in that instant to an understanding of the uses to which the Bureau has put them, but he pushes this away, not able, as he never will be, to confront what the Bureau has made of him. But I must do it, I must do the best for her that I can because, well, because that is what is expected of me and I must always meet my obligations. He is obsessed with the thought that his obligations must be fulfilled; in a simpler age he would have been a slave to duty.

"Oh, now it is coming," Lena says, "it is coming upon me hard and fast, I can feel it growing within, do not abandon me now nor let me fail, but rather penetrate me more deeply, more darkly, until at last suspension is over and all is done." John, not unwillingly, humps and jumps over her, rising and sinking to various heights and depths, the surfaces of his body gleaming with the honesty of his efforts as underneath Lena begins to twitch and contract. "Here it is," she says, "here it is now and now and now and known again," and, in a falling scream, goes into her small and at last silent spasms which are all that she will ever know of pleasure, nipples gleaming, teeth gleaming, eyes flat and widened, and she climaxes with a groan, reaches her hands toward him, puts her fingers in his shoulders as if she were adjusting various levers shipside and sets off again. Patiently, doing the best that he can, John stalks her.

If these passages give the impression that Lena is not attractive, they have been poorly handled, because the fact is that she is quite beautiful. The aesthetic standards of this age are very close to those of our own, history tending to reenact itself more often than not, history having an impoverished invention, and Lena would certainly compare well with a movie star of the late 1950s to the middle 1960s, before anachronisms invaded our own life cycle. She has huge breasts, a tiny waist, full lips, lush thighs, large nipples which stand up under the most superficial kind of titillation. . . . She is, in sum, wildly attractive in terms of those sexual obsessions which framed the author, and perhaps a few of his fantasies have slid into the confrontation here.

The author is not being prurient. I can no more imagine myself having intercourse with Lena than I could conceive of myself as being in *Skipstone;* it is all detached in the extreme. I am not one of those writers whose creations become so vital to him that he literally laughs, weeps, argues, confers with them. My literary influences are more Russian than Mediterranean, so to speak, and I can therefore derive only the slightest prurient feedback from the depiction of Lena.

Nor, the contract with the reader being firm, is this description for prurient release upon the reader either. The author has other and far easier devices of arousal and so, for that matter, do his publishers; I refer you to the rack of books slightly to the right of here and above eye level if you are seeking an easy release and good luck to you as well; I have surely been there myself in one guise or another. No, Lena's beauty is more cleansing than sensual; she is one of those women who induce reverence rather than lust, at least with the majority of partners, and I can offer no better evidence of this than how little pleasure John is really obtaining from sex with her. This is a profound commentary not only upon his character—which is in many ways more interesting than hers and it is a pity, accordingly, that he is a minor figure in this novel—but upon the society from which both of them have evolved. For here sex is little more than a medium of social exchange, an extension of the contract which all humans make with one another to give no pain, at least superficially, unless forced, and far more could be read into this coupling than is truly there. Sex is not that important in the fortieth century, although it is important enough to make possible even here, even then, their own kind of pornography.

Regardless. John is able at last to achieve his orgasm; with a whine and cry so feeble that he might be a child, he tumbles in and out of her, falls away so that Lena, clutching at him, still seeking that last lunge of his which will touch off her final satisfaction (but she will not find it and would not have found it if he had stayed atop her for an hour), gives a bleat of anguish as he revolves upon the pallet to look through the dome and then, putting her disappointment aside, turns onto her own back. She is a controlled woman, she has a sense of proportion about these matters and knows the triviality of seeking orgasm.

"I'm afraid of the dead," she says.

It is as if they have not copulated at all. She merely picks up on the conversation. "I'm frightened of them," she says again as if John had argued with her. "I have a right to feel that way if I want to feel that way."

"You shouldn't be."

"I don't want to go with them. They have no right to make them cargo."

"They become companions in space," John says. These are indeed the reports brought back by commanders of the other FTL craft, that at times they feel that they are close to the dead, that there is a true communion, space being so alien that living and dead are more possessed of the humanity that once touched them than separated by mortality. "If anything you will be glad to have them there. And if things get too bad you have the prostheses to keep you company, to talk to."

John wonders vaguely why he is arguing this point with Lena. Any pilot who so resists the conditions of the voyage should be relieved of the command; that is the policy that he would adopt if he had any true influence. He does not, however; he is merely another functionary of the Bureau and the Bureau's dictates are quite clear, have been explained to him: it is absolutely imperative that Lena take the *Skipstone*. Too much has been invested in her for command to be shifted now.

"That's the other thing," she is saying. "The prostheses *aren't* company. Metallic frames. Machines which work on tape. They're horrible."

"But they have the personalities and the memories of some very wonderful people, skilled technicians, counselors, advisers, supportive people who can—"

"That doesn't matter. They're still machines. Dead and machines in space; that's all that they give me."

"Lena," John says, although this disturbs him, too; he has long thought that the craft should be dual-controlled even though the Bureau insists that the costs and the intrapersonal tensions would be unmanageable, "they can't send more than one live person into space. That's always been the case. The support systems would not carry more than one person. Within those limits, Bureau is trying their best." He is careful to say *Bureau*. Under normal role-provisions he would say *we*, but increasingly John is separating himself from the Bureau in his mind. He does not agree with how it has handled Lena's preparations. More than before, he is severely disturbed by what he feels to be a lack of comprehension on its part of her real anguish, an anguish he is beginning to apprehend. "They want you to be happy."

"But I'm not happy."

"Happiness is not that necessary," John says reasonably. "No one empowers us to be happy; it is not part of your training, not part of our life. All that is necessary is that you be able to handle the circumstances of the voyage and in that regard Bureau has done its best."

"I know that," she says a little sullenly, "I know that; I realize what you're saying, but it isn't fair, John, it just isn't right," and she goes on then to make certain statements about the Bureau, express certain opinions of what she thinks it has made the true purpose of her mission which are perhaps best excluded from the text of the novel since they are, let us understand this, merely the paranoid outpourings of a young woman who is under a good deal of strain, who possesses only modest intellectual gifts and whose emotional state has begun to buckle under the impact of the voyage and her realization of its importance. If there were anything useful in these meanderings, the author would be the first to put them down (and John, he says to himself, would be the first to report them to the Bureau; he would have no choice; he would have to tell them everything because that is his responsibility, but he does not think that there is anything significant here; he wishes to believe that).

Also beside the point would be text on what happens later, how John and Lena in these last days before the flight of *Skipstone* stumble into a slightly deeper emotional relationship, how John manages to find her desirable after all, how certain commitments are stressed in their final coupling which, although instantly forgotten the day the ship departs, are taken very seriously by both at the time that they are said.

And, since it falls outside Lena's point of view, it will not be necessary to describe John's uneasy relationship with the Bureau, the careful reports he hands it almost daily, the intimate and terrible nature of his confessions. To probe his mind superficially is one thing, but to reproduce these confessions is quite another. In order to approach the material, I would have to use full multiple point of view—a largely discredited technique which can only work in odd snippets and flashes—or worse yet the archaic, omniscient author, and although there has been a little of both here, *Galaxies* really needs a more intense focus, a narrowing. Multiple points of view are obviously unacceptable.

Suffice it to say that John omits discussion of Lena's mental state from his reports, that the Bureau, in any case, files those reports without reading, keeping them merely as a procedural hedge against *Skipstone*'s failure so that there will be someone to blame. It would be John's fault for not reporting emotional or psychic inadequacies to his superiors, the Bureau would say. John feels somewhat guilty for omitting the many disturbing things that Lena has said, but this guilt is hardly to the point where he would leave anything out of the reports that he felt the Bureau really ought to know. Instead he discusses her sexual behavior, material which he knows has never failed to interest the clerks. (He would be most distressed to know that nothing interests the clerks and that his reports are unread.)

Of Lena's relationship with John little more will be made of here, but it is one of those details which come upon her as she relives her life while falling into the neutron star and should be included on that account. By no means has the material been incorporated for the sake of prurience, since the sexual material is relevant to understanding Lena.

XXIII

Many years ago I appeared in concert on a radio talk show attended by two grim-faced men representing the Citizens' League for Decent Literature who were attempting to hold a Mother's Day rally in a local stadium celebrating, with the help of bicyclists and Miss Teenage America, the temporarily outflanked but risen-to-anger forces of virtue. "The thing that I hold against pornography," one of the grim-faced men pointed out, "is that any hack can write it, any *hack* can turn out a scene describing sex and the human body and create a perverted interest, but that isn't *writing*. That isn't *art*. That isn't what a *novel* is all about."

I raged toward the microphone to destroy the grim-faced Decent Citizen with an aphorism which would wrap him into the wire, but as I started to speak, I realized that I agreed with him. The man was right. "I agree with you. You are right," I said. The Decent Citizen smiled. "But, of course, the First Amendment covers all that," I added hastily. The Decent Citizen smiled again. The Mother's Day rally, however, fell through. Not enough financial support from the public.

XXIV

As *Skipstone* dives, the relationship with John is merely one of the events which pass stately across the panels of Lena's mind. There are many others, events that is, and if I were interested in a little discreet padding, I would have no difficulty in filling many pages with exposition. Lena's whole life could be placed here in a terse but endless number of scenes, dropped in to bulk up the word count. (Any professional learns things like this almost before he has started selling.) I could flash back and flash forward, depict Lena at work and at play in many postures through her young life, could feed in colorful dramatic snippets which would illuminate the strange and wonderful nature of the society from which she comes. There are at least twelve thousand words available here, and perhaps I would be a fool not to do it, depending, of course, on how short the novel would look in first draft. There may be enough already. Then again the book may be short and under deadline pressure, and I may have to add those twelve thousand words. It all depends. Everything depends. It is a wholly dependent universe except in the matter of morality where there may be certain absolutes.

Fortunately this is merely a set of notes for a novel and not the novel itself, and therefore I should not have to concern myself with what will be padding and what will not be. I can put in precisely what I want, what will advance the plot and no more. There is little plot in these early moments of falling, and therefore the material will be held down.

Then, too, I am not terribly interested in Lena or her society. They have little to do with what is going on here which could be at any time. . . . I only want to posit a technology which makes possible FTL craft that can find the neutron stars. The word for this 3902 is *arid*. It is hard to conceive that a system which could populate the numerous stars could be homogenous, rigid, dull and puritanical, but that is really what humanity has become, even though it numbers fifty billions on one hundred and seven separate worlds, moons and asteroids. The polyglot variety of our time, which comes from relatively high social mobility and institutions in decay, is really an aberrant event in man's history. Institutions tend to stabilize and control; socioeconomic levels tend to stratify. Goods are distributed unequally by heredity; religious or state sanctions merely function to keep the system in place. The years from 1900 through 2155 happen to mark one of those infrequent periods of our history when this was not the case, because the technological devices are far ahead of the ability of the culture to absorb them; but 3902 is deep in a period of stability. Under the hand of the Bureau which controls everything related to space, there have been no conflicts in several hundred years, except for minor disputes between governments of colonies too widely separated to engage in warfare.

The Bureau should not be thought of as tyrannical—it merely occupies a place; it is a quality of the environment. Those in its service have no sense of being oppressors, nor does the Bureau adopt the attitudes of the totalitarian.

These are dull times. Despite the infinite variety which they would seem to have for us, the people of the fortieth century find them unremarkable and similarly dull. Because of the functionality of the system, the tight integration of institutions and individuals, most are rather well compensated. It is just as well that this is so and that Lena has been drawn from a pool of people even more stable than the norm. Thirty seconds in FTL would drive any of our contemporary astronauts mad. A month under the devices of the Bureau would give any of us severe social illness. Different times, different conditions . . . the gladiators would not have done very well in the New York subway system.

This all taken into account, there will be little time spent on explication of Lena's past life. Lena is as unremarkable as most of her contemporaries, and her training has acted to flatten her further, it being sickening, repetitive, technical and dull. Material could be put in for padding if conditions forced, but it would seem better to pad the novel in other areas, areas in which the extraneous material could react more vitally with its theme.

For instance, as the ship falls, there could be some elaboration on the suggestion that neutron stars might be pulsars which would be most intriguing, if the reader has not been intrigued sufficiently already by the notion that all of "life" as we understand it when we glimpse the heavens may be merely an incidental by-product of the cycle of neutron stars.

So *there*, Cheever, Barth, Barthelme, Oates. What in the collected works would touch *that* for *angst?*

XXV

Pulsars occur on spectrographs or other sophisticated receivers as rhythmic messages from space, messages which may be defined as light or sound but which have no visual counterpart. In short, their signals give evidence of their existence, but they cannot be seen, which, in the early days of their discovery, led to the theory that they might indeed be coded messages sent by intelligent aliens.

Later it was found that the pulsars do not emanate from single stars but are probably impulses received from entire galaxies, galaxies so many light-years distant that they can be traced by no telescopic equipment available and which are indeed so unimaginably far that their light may not yet have reached us, may not yet reach us for billions of years, although they may well have a history equivalent to our own.

New theories suggest that, while some of the pulsars may be galaxies, others may represent the dying neutron stars or, then again, a neutron star in collapse might *become* a galaxy. What we receive, then, are messages of the imminent collapse of the universe. The neutron stars chatter out their little warnings in clear spectrographic pattern. This concept, that the pulsars are the squalling of failed stars, causes anguish. This possibility would not be evaded during the course of *Galaxies*, and the period of *Skipstone*'s fall would be the proper place of insertion, since it is here, finally, where all the strands of the novel meet, no tension at the center, all of it in the filigree and dark of its suggestion.

XXVI

And then, too, this is Lena's novel. The focus must be kept on her; it would serve no purpose to wander further from her because to the degree that *Galaxies* generates power, it will come from its portrait of the protagonist who is the filter of all impressions. So let it be known, let it be taken into account, that all of the time that *Skipstone* is falling, Lena is in terrible pain. She is suffering. Her anguish is real and her desolation barely a measure of her fear.

For this novel is about people. Evolution is about people; so are neutron stars, pulsars and even the machinations of the Bureau: at the center is always the frail, human form under the lash of brutality or the light-years, and in the hold of the ship which falls interminably in a flight which may go on forever because not only light but time is contained by gravitation. Lena is screaming. She comes in and upon herself over and over again, ripped from end to end, her joints like sealing wax, her eyes torn out like water, lots not being cast over her vestments only because she has no vestments, and there is no one alive, no one alive in the hold of the ship to cast lots over her. But this will come. All of this will happen to her, and since she knows not only the past but the future, she sees this, and it adds to her anguish, although she cannot express it. She can express nothing. She merely holds and falls.

And falling she sees the dead, falling she hears them, the dead address her from the hold and they, too, are screaming. In this new gravitation, the dead and the living have, as John has predicted, merged, the dead not knowing their condition nor the living, everything the same; meat distended, and yet the old distinction somehow holds if only in attitude, for the dead are other than Lena and they shout.

They shout: "Release us, release us, we are alive. What is happening? We are in terrible pain. What is happening? Why are we in such torment?" and so on and so forth, their many voices speaking with one through the hold, revolving speech marking passage from one to the other, poor baffled creatures coming to consciousness after centuries of empti-ness in a condition which means that every dream that they have ever known of horror has come true. (Perhaps this is the secret of death itself; we live in the hope of a merciful God who looks upon us with benevolence, but what do we know of the disposition of souls or what is planned for us?) So there they lie, there in that gelatinous flux, their distended limbs sutured finger and toe to the membranes which have held them. Their decay has, if not reversed, at least been halted and imploded as the neutron star has itself imploded; the warp into which they have fallen has reversed time so that now they are alive (or at least they are not-dead), and they beg Lena to release them from anguish which they cannot express, so profound is it.

The voices are in her head, they peal and bang like oddly shaped bells and where, oh, where, is she? She does not know. She has no sense of partition but seems, instead, to exist in all space.

"Release us," they scream. "We are no longer dead; the trumpet has sounded and we have been raised; we have been raised incorruptible in a moment, in the twinkling of an eye, at the last trumpet!" and so on and so forth; perhaps they do not shout this but some other theological scrap or snippet, but this is how their cries are referred to Lena who is familiar with some of the old texts. She knows, then, she knows exactly what is happening and maintains consciousness of what has occurred, but then again, she does *not*, there is no circumstantial function. In the larger sense she is aware, but in the matter of particular she is not.

Not only the issue of her pain holds her here. She is merely the ferryman on this passage, not a medical specialist, and she knows nothing of the mysteries of return, of the effect of supergravitational properties upon the corpus of the dead. All that she knows of those dead is that their passage through hyperspace has, in some way unknown to her, changed the very ions of which they are constituted so that they will be in a state of preanimacy and that the process will be further extended upon their return. This is the very latest and most sophisticated of all the experiments in unlocking the dead which have been going on for several hundred years, and although it has returned a scattering of them to perilous life, the expense of carrying them as cargo has been so high, the chances of their continued animation (most of the restored die for a second and final time very quickly) so slight, that the process can be considered to be only at its most rudimentary stages. It may be a false pursuit which will then be abandoned. On all the planets and galaxies no more than twenty of the previous dead exist, and their lives can hardly be said to be satisfactory, since their chemistry has become so precarious that they exist only in tanks, immobilized. Was it for this that they willed enormous sums to have themselves preserved hundreds of years ago? Lena cannot possibly answer this. She cannot speak for them.

She could not, in any event, grant them release. Despite their cries, their vows of life restored, their departure from the medium which nourishes them would surely destroy. She would explain this to them if only she could, take it patiently step by step through the process of causing them to know what has happened, but her technical knowledge is entirely too slender and she has succumbed to her own responses.

Those responses overwhelm her.

For here, in this black hole, if the dead indeed are risen (and this is a question which the novel just cannot confront, staggering in the thin and shrinking line between metaphysics and science where little but the hope for rationality can be said to exist), then the risen can be considered the dead. For she, too, dies in this space. She dies a thousand times over a period of seventy thousand years. There is no objective time here; chronology is controlled only by the psyche, and so Lena has a thousand full lives, a thousand individual and richly textured deaths, and it is awful of course as only something like this can be, but it is also interesting, because for every cycle of death there is also a life. Seventy thousand years, one thousand times seventy upon which she may meditate, if not reenact, her condition.

XXVII

And this is a concept so broad, so (as the old pulp magazines might have billed it) mind-shattering, that it is worth considering for just a little while. As the ship, past its initial lurch into the field of the neutron star, becomes part of the black galaxy, as the ship partakes of the energies and properties of a gravitation so immense, Lena begins to live not only her life again, but also the life of various separate identities which are not hers.

Some of these are identities transferred from the dead in the hold, others are taken from those that she has known in her previous life and others still (like this novel itself) have been completely constructed, fictional lives that nevertheless have all the reality and omnipresence of truth. Self-invention, spontaneous creation are as pervasive as anything that has happened, Lena finds, and as she lives a thousand lives over these seventy thousand years (give or take a few years overall and falling well within the Bell Curve of chances), she has the time to find out a great deal.

It is quite painful. It would have to be this way. Who can possibly describe or imagine what it would be like to live seventy years in solitude, let alone one thousand times seventy, let alone the complete recall of all the previous lives available to the present? There is simply no language for this within the present, and although the author's technical resources are well to the level of any of his peers, he would not even make the attempt. It is simply beyond him. Before something like this, a decent sense of awe must be kindled.

But it can be said that the black galaxy not only repeats and intensifies time, but also compresses so that although seventy thousand years are in one sense quite extended, in another they are short enough for Lena to undergo all of the sensations of her various lives in what she knows—as a dreamer might be able to make assessment outside his dreams—to be a shorter span. Knowledge and memory are not so much enacted through her as implanted. She knows in every way what those seventy lives were like, then, but it is a knowledge of recollection rather than partaking, much as one might stagger from a dream, recollecting for the instant all of its myriad details without, however, having experienced them. What can one say? The black hole, like dreams, destroys time.

Here, in short, is the point at which the novel could be extended. To put it another way, it could be padded out to almost any length demanded by the publisher. One could conceive of a whole cycle of novels here, a *recherché pas du space age*, seventy volumes interrelated, each of them dealing with another of Lena's lives, all of them locked together by the prologue—title it *Before the Black Galaxy*—and the novel of epilogue which would conclude everything in a fulfilled and satisfying manner. An author with a modicum of energy, a modest scale of expenses and moderate pretensions might well be able to draw a publisher's advance on this scheme for the rest of his working life, for, in the way that all series in genre fiction can be said to be, these novels would be self-reinforcing. The audience would build from book to book as well as send its newer readers in search of the earlier works of the series.

So, then, one could compose a work which would span the centuries and the world, which would describe all of human history in chiaroscuro from the present day or a little earlier right through the year 3902, and the series would mesh cleverly, since a character in one novel could share certain memories and events with characters in the other, a complex, towering fugal arrangement which would keep the author lunging from novel to subsequent novel until, in simple exhaustion, from audience apathy or in search of better things to do, the author would abandon the series in midcareer. Or drive it to a fast conclusion: Lena rescued from the black hole, *Skipstone* falls through and out the other end, Lena resigns herself to an eternity of plunge and so on. There would be as many ways to finish it off, in short, as to expand, and even at a relatively modest advance, the author would find the temptation hard to put off. Security and the middle class beckoning. As Lena's problems multiply so could the author's be said to have come under control.

This, however, is not the line that *Galaxies* would take. Put it down not to an excess of integrity nor laziness: I simply do not want the work moving in that direction. The point, after all, is not what happens to Lena as a side effect of her fall but what she does to get out of her predicament and what effect those struggles have not only upon her own consciousness, but also upon that of the reader. The true basis of the novel, then, would not be found in the side effects which are merely peripheral to these basic points.

Besides, the author confesses to a certain boredom. His own life is at least as difficult to manage as Lena would find her seventy; too much of his energy is involved with assuming mastery of his own existence. Why create false proposals? *Galaxies* will assume Lena's multiple lives without undue explication and leave the reader, that collaborator, to judge the effects of all this upon her.

Sufficient to say that, although Lena is neither stupid nor insensitive, she is not one of the strongest personalities available in this culture. If she were, she would not be in what is essentially a technician's job. (The effect of the multiple existences upon her thus might be crushing, but then again it might only inspirit her to a deeper characteriological and metaphysical framework than she had ever known previously.) Who is to say? There are certain areas which even science fiction writers are not equipped to explore with any certainty, and before the mysterious curtains which shroud the one, discrete human soul, it may be best, after all, to stay silent.

XXVIII

Galaxies, having set up its background, having reached its crisis early on (in conformation with the basic principles of good plotting), would then plunge into its basic argument and conflict which would occur when Lena at last decides that she must summon help. She must obtain from the prostheses an evaluation, or, failing that, she must in some way establish communication with the dead.

Now, the fact that it has taken her seventy thousand years to reach this decision is in one way incredible, and yet in another and more significant way it is simple and miraculous. In an infinite universe, possibilities similarly multiplied, only a fraction of them reconstituted even now, it is highly unlikely that even once in seventy thousand years of lives and reenactments she would have intercepted a personality which would seek help in this way, and had it not been for the fact that she is unusually strong-willed and that the personality which she inhabits is so weak that she can override it, it might not have happened yet—*Skipstone* and its denizens might be plunging onward instead of having reached a point of resolution which, later on, we will be able to explicate.

Before she has summoned the prostheses, Lena has had time to think, and she decides that the prostheses might provide her with the only set of answers. There has been an accretion of memory from life to life so that she has been able to do some almost conterminous thinking, and when the moment comes when she may act, she is prepared to do so.

Some of her previous personalities have also been weak but not in this way, in a fashion to encourage override. Others have been strong, not a few have been insane, but there has been a little residue even in the worst of them to carry forth the knowledge of what she must do, and so in the seventy thousandth and first year, when the cumulative truth of the matter has come upon her, Lena realizes what has happened and what will happen next and what she must do to deal with this.

She summons all of her strength and will. She is, in this thousandth existence, occupying the persona of a sniveling, whining old man of the 3200s who had enough money to embalm but not quite enough to seal off his body from relatives who, for profit, put it on exhibition in their temple for many years as an artifact and the center of a sect, until one by one the members of the family left the temple, the cult fell into disgrace and the institutions of the time began to confiscate its property. Meanwhile the corpus was immaculately preserved, the society of all times having had one consistency: to protect and perpetuate the bodies of the embalmed so that they could enjoy the possibility of revival.

In this persona she summons John. As he did not tell her until the very moment of her embarkation, his personality is also on *Skipstone*, one of the prostheses, implanted within a metallic block approximately but not truly in the shape of a man. (It was deliberate that the prostheses not appear human. It prevents the ferryman, who may at the time of summoning be in a near-psychotic stage, from reacting to them as if they were people; at one time there were some terrible incidents which need not be described here.) Sensors turn, little lights and wiring play, and as the machine whirs, coughing into the block the preserved persona of John, Lena gasps in relief, too weak even to respond with pleasure to the fact that in this condition of null time, canceled light, ruined causality, the machinery still works!

But, then, the machinery would. It would function. Even in this final and most dreadful of situations, the machinery continues to function. This has always been the point of science fiction: that if we did not master the future, it would be from our own incapacities and never those of the machines. They may have been right, they may have been wrong, but those old science fiction writers had one core insight: whatever happened would eventually devolve upon technology. Fail in that and everything fails.

"Hello," John says within a shimmering, silver block, crudely sculptured into a parody of human form, little blind lights winking at one end, little extensions balancing at the other. "I'm glad to see you."

Fully implanted with the personality and memories of he who has been obtained, the prosthesis assumes at this moment of summoning the condition of her superior. Of course it is *not* John. Lena must remember this at all times and also must know that the prosthesis has no memory of the voyage. Its recollections have been shut off from the time that John fed the log of his personality, piece by aching piece, into the receptors during the weeks before the voyage. She cannot, then, fall upon this contrivance and beg for salvation. It would literally not know what she was talking about; it is there to provide technical and humanitarian assistance only to the point that information can be given to it. That is true, Lena says to herself, moving her lips, subvocalizing these assurances; that is true, I must remember this at all times, I must not think that this thing is human.

This knowledge is wrenching, and the old man with whom she shares the cavern of consciousness is similarly distressed and somehow she maintains enough control to keep the two in balance, to maintain her sense of control and identity and to address John in a slow, reasonable tone. This is no small accomplishment. It cannot be dismissed easily. Possibly I have underestimated Lena to this point. She is showing a kind of behavioral control and absolute discipline which would be beyond anyone of this time and highly exceptional even in hers.

"What is the matter, Lena?" John says. He knows—it knows, whatever the device may be called—that he would only be summoned if there were some kind of serious trouble in flight. "Can you tell me what's wrong? What can I do for you?" Her mentor would have phrased it just this way, yet—in the context—it seems absolutely stupid to her.

And the blundering nature of this question, its naïveté and irrelevance in the midst of what she has occupied, stuns Lena, and yet more when she compares this mask to the actual John who would never (well, would he? could he be this way?) act so stupidly, but she realizes even through the haze of blockage that this John would, of course, join her without any memory of immediate circumstance. He would have to be told what is happening. He knows nothing at all.

Inevitably, then, she must brief him. It is hard to maintain control over that other personality which once again has panicked and is scrambling desperately against the walls of consciousness, trying to get out of there, trying to find sleep once again but of course it cannot, not until the genetic allotment of its mortality has been exhausted. She must reassert her own personality. Whining and sniveling she manages to brief the thing that is John, half in one voice, half in another, as to what has happened.

(Some comment should be made on background: the awful stillness of the ship in the fall, an absolute cancellation of motion, even a placidity in the grip of collapse which gives an almost pastoral stillness to the interior whose support systems continue to function. It also should be clearly stated that seventy thousand years is *subjective* time to Lena; no such period has actually elapsed. No time at all can be said to have passed since the fall began, and the biological systems are frozen. Naturally she could not have survived seventy thousand years or even seventy thousand seconds in plunge. All event is perceived only through the engineering which controls the subjective time-belt; it is by no means implied that the objective passage of time can be measured at all.)

Lena does know what has happened. A thousand lives, seventy thousand years, have enabled her to reconstruct, quite painfully but piece by piece, the cosmology which has put her in this position. It has not been easy, but then again in seventy thousand years of thought almost anyone could reconstruct the cosmos. This, in any event, is the premise of the novel, take or leave its essential optimism as you will. She tells John, then, about the neutron star, about the implosion which has brought her to this condition, about gravitation. About light and pain. John in metallic frame stands there quietly, listening to this. Indeed there is little else that he can do; the prostheses are triggered only by pauses in conversation, will otherwise stand mute, and Lena's jumble of recollection, explanation and hysteria goes on without pause. Finally she is done, and when it is certain that this is so, the device moves its rudimentary head in what might be a very human gesture or then again might only represent its projection by Lena of her need to have it be human.

"Remarkable," it says.

"Yes."

"That's really remarkable. And terrible, of course. You've shown a great deal of strength in being able to assess the situation."

"Yes."

"And not to panic. That's remarkable also. You've met this test with real strength." The programs, of course, are slanted to be encouraging and supportive, this being Bureau's conception of how users might best be served. "You're a remarkable woman. I'm really proud of you. Then, too, you have a right to be proud of yourself. Are you? I truly hope you are."

"That has nothing to do with anything," Lena says. "You've got to help me."

"You say that this falling continues still? That at this moment we're diving?"

"Falling now, falling forever."

"How terrible for you."

Lena looks at the blank masking which covers the portholes, wondering what would happen now if she were to strip that masking away so that she could see the black hole itself. She does not think that she could bear it, and yet at some point, even past seventy thousand years, she knows that she will have to do it. The compulsion is absolute.

"Would you care to talk some more about your feelings, Lena? Why don't you talk?"

"You've got to help me," she says. "This has nothing to do with feelings."

"What would you like me to do? What do you think that I *could* do? How long have you had these feelings that you could derive help from me, Lena? Do you really think that the solution lies outside yourself?"

"You've got to have a function," she says. "All of you were placed here in order to help with some emergency; this is an emergency. Do something. Tell me what can be done to end this."

"Well, now," John says, "well, now, Lena, let's consider that a little if we may." It addresses her with superb calm which has also been programmed in, the only emotion which is picked up on the tapes. It would hardly be supportive, the Bureau has long since calculated, to have prostheses capable of other emotions on these flights; they would lead to vast complications far beyond the ability of the Bureau itself to contain. At one time it was argued at the highest levels that emotions of warmth, affection, passion might meet the program, but in the end it had been decided against, since none of them would serve any technological purpose.

"Let us consider," the prosthesis is saying. "I could hardly help you, although I know that to you I represent a factor that you always looked to for help. Still, the means for release are beyond me."

"Are they?"

"If beyond you, beyond me," John points out. "That would stand to reason, wouldn't it?"

"But you've got to have an answer! You were installed to be called upon, so that you could help."

"Only in those matters which would fall within my experience," John says with a little regret. "Really, I am little more than a mechanical contrivance, a data bank as it were which can give you faster access to facts of a certain kind than you could obtain by research. I mean I'm perfectly willing to be supportive—that's what we're here for after all, to render support—but you'd be wrong in looking at me as much more than a catalog or perhaps a synthesis of information. So you see I'm not capable of that kind of action."

"You must be."

"But I'm not." Although the crude metal is not designed for expression, she seems to think that John is betraying grief, but this is undoubtedly emotional; she is being emotional once again. "I'm truly not."

"Impossible."

"Not impossible. Objective fact. In truth your problem is that you are projecting on me certain emotional needs which I cannot possibly fulfill."

"Emotional needs?"

"Of course. I am not your mentor, your lover John, but merely a representation of his personality, a simulacrum of this real person who is certainly not at all here."

"I know that."

"But perhaps you are not sure. At an emotional level, Lena, you may be shielding yourself from this fact. Be honest with yourself. You did not call upon me for intellectual advice but emotional support, and I cannot yield that at all."

Consider this: they tumble into a black hole in an eternity of pain and yet the prosthesis is engaging in elemental casework procedure. Surely this appears confusing to the reader—how, after all, can the sense of wonder be congealed with the principles of modern social work?—but this is among the points the novel has to make; that the Bureau's attack upon the universe has been to obliterate its pain and hence its parameters by acting as if it could be handled with routine techniques of therapeutic approach which have not changed at all in two thousand years, have merely become ritualized.

"You're going to have to deal with this yourself, Lena," the metallic thing points out. "There is quite little that the cyborg technique can do for you; you can no longer displace the responsibility for your condition upon machines. In fact I seem to recall raising this very point in discussions at the Bureau a long, long time ago, but no one ever listened to me. They never listened at all there."

"What are you talking about?" Lena says. "I have no idea what you're saying." This is only a partial truth. She knows quite well indeed what is being suggested—that she is alone, that she is in a void, that this metal merely simulates companionship and that no one can save her—but at the level of emotional acceptance she has indeed become blank. Something impenetrable within her through all the subjective centuries of pain has finally shifted, and she now feels open in a way which hardly dignifies her. "Help me," she says again.

"I can't."

"You must. Otherwise this will go on forever."

There is, here, a pathos which I cannot really transmit. Open sentiment has never been one of my virtues; the ironic sense is too strong for me to bring off a scene at the level of simple emotional clarity which gives sentiment its often despised power. I could say that what gives this scene much of its horror is that Lena yearns toward a lover whose very form mocks that yearning, a form the Bureau has designed to parody that emotion. "Oh," she says, "if you don't help me, who will? Who can?"

"There are others," the device says. "Engineers, tutors, advisors are also in the bank, and they might be able to give you more practical advice, although I doubt this. But there's no reason for you to feel that everything begins and ends here; truly it does not have to. It's merely your emotional condition running away with you."

"I hate you," she says then. "I hate you."

"Don't hate me. I am merely an abstraction; that would get you nowhere. Get hold of yourself."

"I have hold of myself. I hate you now."

"You can only find these feelings of hatred destructive. In any case," the cyborg continues, "the situation as you've put it is frightening and upsets me no less than it does you. In fact, although no decent machine should ever confess to something like this, I'm beginning to feel my own balance starting to disappear. This is a very tenuous creation here, weak and frozen circuitry, levels of fusion which can hardly put up with any severe stress. I am going to disconnect."

"You can't do that."

"Of course I can do that. Don't be silly; I can do anything that I want. We have a complete range of free-willed choices available to us; we can regulate our own participation. Otherwise we would be dominated and utilized in such a way as to make yourself quite mad. By free will I must detach myself before something drastic happens, and of course I obey it absolutely."

The cyborg labors in a rather clumsy way toward one of the portholes and lifts its tentacles to part the curtains.

Lena can do nothing. She is astonished by the action, does not understand it and yet unwillingly, as she stares, she begins to see the sense. She can see what the cyborg has said to her and realize that it is quite right: it could hardly bear this staggering situation. It was not made for it; Bureau did not anticipate black galaxies or their interception when the lists for *Skipstone* were compiled. She had no right to expect anything; it was foolishness even to summon, but then again, what choice did she have? What could she have done? She needed help and thought that it could be provided here, and the weakness, then, is not that of the cyborg but her own. She must understand this. She remains in place as the thing rolls to a porthole, tears open the curtains and takes a long look at the aspect glinting through, an aspect which Lena herself will not witness even though she has seen it in her mind for seventy thousand years; she will not look at it, and then a cry both human and metallic emerges from the thing at the porthole.

It bellows in a pain which might be pleasure so acute is the sound, and then the very joints seem to decompose (although Lena knows that this must be, it would have to be, an illusion; sight could not destroy steel nor could sensation alone break an engine, could it? Could this happen?), and then it leans and staggers against a bulkhead, arches in upon itself and collapses. It does not, after that first stricken bellow, make any sound at all, as if all feeling had been drawn from it on that one single line. Lena manages to stand, move in that direction and, her hand become a tentacle, her eyes closed, she seizes the curtain and draws it closed, shutting off the light and the death of the black galaxy, and then she is alone.

"I am alone," she says with just a hint of self-dramatization (but she can be pardoned this); I am alone, she thinks, and knows that she is not, not in any sense which will profit her. Because somewhere below her the cyborg that was once John lies, but she neither sees nor touches; instead her body shrinks and then she scuttles away. The personality of the dead with which her persona has shared this momentarily becomes the stronger, and she begins to whine and mumble then like an old incontinent, shudder within the container of her flesh as if it were despicable, and this may go on for years and then again it may go on for moments (there is no time in the black galaxy, except the time that she feels has elapsed; time is a function of condition), but eventually, like all things, it stops, and she must confront her basic problem again. Always she will have to do this.

She is alone in the ship. Her descent continues. Her pain does not remit. She is out of control and yet she is in control. Nothing can be understood and yet in another way all is comprehensible. All. All can be known. Something must be done. She cannot bear this eternally.

XXIX

And here could run yet another moody flashback concerning Lena's relationship with John, dropped in to provide color and poignancy, augmenting the mood of despair. Long sexual passages here could alternate with painful streams of consciousness in the present. Sex and space, orgasm and isolation could run counterpoint, and the author's gifts for irony, which are not modest, would be exhibited to their fullest range. Also, in the traditions of modern science fiction, the sex scenes could be quite titillating, render the novel some extra-literary interest. A construct like this could use all the extra-literary interest it could get.

But this would not work. *Space is asepsis:* straddling this simple and irrevocable insight, the temptation to write long and easy scenes of coupling falls to ash. How can I show sex, even retrospectively, against a background where light and history are themselves contained?

I cannot. I would not even attempt it; that is all there is to say about the matter, and in addition to this Lena's thoughts have already veered far from John. They are less retrospectively concerned than fixed on the immediacy and difficulty of her situation, the need to deal with it and obtain escape.

She wants to change her condition. She wants to get out of this. Of course she does, how natural a need; but consider the measure of her entrapment in that it has taken seventy thousand years for her to have reached this point of decision. There are monolithic writers and those who pace slowly, but even a Jamesian standard weakens by comparison here. This is a character who has taken a thousand selves and seventy times that to decide that her situation is unbearable. Science fiction must truly be a superior medium if it can involve such an extension, such a superimposition of leisurely pace upon material. Nothing else in any other form could begin to approach it.

Still, if it is understood that the black galaxy does indeed contain time as well as light and sensation, memory as well as all sub-FTL speeds, then it is not unreasonable that it would take Lena this long to reach any point of decision. Indeed, it is quite a substantial declaration that she would come through all of these stresses alive. There is nobody of our time who could have survived what has happened, yet training methods and the undoubted factor of evolution have produced many Lenas, individuals whose capacity for experience and the weight it bears goes far beyond our own. They can, in our terms, tolerate anything. Governments throughout history, in fact, have sought a population with Lena's patience and malleability; to many of them she would have been the ideal citizen. Her tolerance levels are quite high.

Nor (because she considers her survival unexceptional, because it is merely a concomitant of her training) can she truly understand the remarkable nature of her survival. She does not consider herself to be an exceptional individual, and this is one of the bitterest of all factors.

The thing that contained John's persona lies near a bulkhead. It makes no gesture. Dead before, it is more dead now, containing nothing. Again she is alone in the ship and overwhelmed once more by the cries of the dead.

XXX

"You were foolish," a dead says to her. "You asked more than could be given."

"I did not."

"Yes, you did. It fit not the programs. There is nothing that they can do for you."

"Then I had no choice. I had to call upon them. I was instructed to call upon them if I needed help."

"Even here you have choices," the dead says. "No matter what your condition, no matter what has happened to you, you exist in a scheme of choice. You must remember this."

The seventy thousand years have had their effect upon the dead as well. At least some of them, it would seem, have learned something. The one to whom she is speaking is extremely patient; he seems to have moved to a new plane of knowledge, but then again the dead may not truly exist in a sentient condition; their apparent existence may simply be a projection of Lena's wild and altered mental state upon their abstraction, or then again the factor of change in the field of the neutron star may make all of her impressions merely hallucinative along with any questions of growth or choice. That would lend *Galaxies* yet another series of levels, of course. The possibility that the acts described may be occurring only as patterns falsely encoded within the protagonist renders everything in it liable to suspicion, although I can give assurance that there are certain poles in this work, that the work can be said to exist in revolution around them. One of the poles is the neutron star and the other is the hypocrisy of the Bureau and the way in which they mesh—becoming, ultimately, the same thing. Also significant is the statement that both Lena and *Skipstone* do exist; they exist at this moment in the sense that all that will be can be said to have already existed, sending back its reverberations to the time before it was created.

"Choices," the dead repeats, since Lena's stream of consciousness has been wandering as it is prone to do. "And you are compelled to make them."

"He did not try to help me."

"He could not have helped you. How could you have expected that he would? You are being very naive; they are not programmed to deal with anything like this."

"I thought he would."

"You are a fool."

"I thought he would help me—"

"*He* is not John. You called upon John but found only a mechanical recreation," the dead says gently. "How can you be brought to realize that what you thought happened did not happen? Everything was based upon a set of false expectations."

"It cannot be."

"It can and it is. If you did not face the truth of the matter, you would not have summoned him. You know where you are and what is happening to us, but you must continue to face that truth, Lena."

"What truth?"

"The truth of resolution. It lies wholly within yourself. Only you may change this."

"How can you say that? How can you tell me that the truth lies within myself? Who are you?" she says and does not know what she is addressing, fearful that she may be talking to herself. "I don't know what qualifies you to say something like this, how you can put on me the responsibility—"

"The truth is the responsibility," the dead says. "And your responsibility is the truth."

And then it says no more. Whether it actually goes away or merely becomes silent when it is finished speaking is something she does not know; she cannot gauge the temper of the dead any more than she can judge the veracity of their address. The murmurs of others surround, the voice blends into all of the voices of the hold and she is shrouded once again in the music and the darkness.

She wanders toward the console again, an action that may take her ten minutes or ten years or (such is the characteristic of time which I am trying to get across here) *both* and looks at it for a while, her fingers trembling. Beside the prosthesis of John in the storage tank lay all of the others, each with its separate abilities and gifts, and she decides to summon them, to try to obtain advice in that way, but the will to call them forth is, for the time, beyond her, and she must gird herself to this for long, struggling instants, because if these cyborgs, too, fail to help her, if they desert her as did John, then she truly does not know if she will be able to contend further with the situation.

Yet. Her desire to survive is still there. Indeed, it must have never left her. It chews away like a rat, busily snipping little raw chunks of personality and she is in its thrall; she is, in fact, astonished by the realization of how desperately she wants to live, somehow to get out of this. It may have been seventy thousand years reaching this point of urgency, but now that it is here it cannot be wasted, she thinks, if they have led to this. She sheds the personality she has inhabited. It falls from her like a cloak and she is once again and fully herself.

Lena places her hands upon the console and summons, simultaneously, three cyborgs.

XXXI

Here the novel obviously veers toward religious allegory, an abused area but one which is obviously inevitable within the difficult context and in terms, too, of the author's personality. Not for nothing has he spent all of those difficult and perilous hours during the period of the High Holy Days, even though it cannot be said that his religious experience is rich in conclusion. Still, for all his ambivalence, complaint and seizures of doubt, the author does not regret his religious affiliation; within his rather secular frame a small and battered *chassid* in cantorial regalia is trying to get out. He will *not* get out, of course; where would he go? There is not a Reform temple in the area which would suit and Orthodoxy is too time consuming, but he will not stay in place either, this *chassid*, and from the tension between his desires and his practice, the author can wring the usual amounts of irony. Nothing at all is easy once you begin to take the thematic subtext seriously, something which applies to science fiction as well as religion. It would be best concentrating on the ritual without excessive attention to its significance. *Slogging Through the Slime Planet* might have been a better investment after all. Ethical Culture certainly involves less than Reform.

But religious disquisition to one side, the allegory will obviously be tempting in that chapter involving the three cyborgs which Lena summons to confer further on her problem. The parallels are indeed clear, and the selection of *three* rather than a single cyborg at a time approaches the level of conscious intention. The resemblance of these summoned to the three comforters of Job could hardly be ignored and would indeed be worked through the material cunningly.

Job. He is that Old Testament figure of faith and submission, or then again he may only be a symbol of cosmic abandonment: God's Fool. For his pains he was subjected by Satan (God having approved the deal with eager curiosity; would Job bend or would he not?) to a series of trials in order to determine whether Job's faith truly came from love of God or merely upon the wealth that God had lavished upon him. Satan in succession lays Job's fields, cattle and children low, leading his wife to suggest that Job curse God and die.

Do not be restless; this is all important. The parable of Job brought the concept of justice into the Old Testament as even Adam's trials did not. Job refuses his wife's demand—although severely tried—and his wife abandons him in disgust. In her place come three wise men from a neighboring province who join him upon the ground to tell sad stories of the death of kings. These are the three comforters, figures of satire, since they fall outside the pain and terror of Satan's vengeance and approach the unspeakable in a burlesque of intellectualism which is, in fact, comic. They give Job the most reasonable, persuasive reasons for his condition and offer reasonable encouragements as to why he should no longer silently bear his grief. They do not prevail, at least not quite, but probably only because the text, like so much of the Old Testament, has been shaped toward the purpose of the didactic. They certainly do not take Job's positions with grace.

In the story of the comforters is the conscious origin of the section in which Lena and the three new prostheses discuss her condition and that of *Skipstone*. Summoned one by one, activated, they are briefed by Lena as she briefed John, and they listen as patiently as that device did, making no interjection. They are not, as I have pointed out, geared toward interruption; their whole supportive presence is for that reason a fraud perpetuated by the Bureau. They are not there to help but merely to grant relief; however, this is the way that the Bureau has always done things on these interstellar sweeps, and who is to say that if it had changed its procedures anything would have been different? Almost assuredly there would have been no difference at all.

None of them is quite as bright as John. This is understandable; John was Lena's supervisor directly on merit. They are, however, bright enough by far to absorb her explanation as well as to understand its seriousness. When she warns them not to go to the portholes, they agree. When she tells them not to look at the galaxy, they do not protest. When she says that the sight of space in this fall will drive even a prosthesis insane, they nod. When she points at the crushed heap of John, they murmur to one another. They construe her remarks correctly, and they do not protest when she says that they must attend to her. And when she is done, they stand in their line of rigid and curious mortification and seem able to say nothing.

"I've now told you everything," she says.

Indeed she has told them everything. They nod solemnly.

"I have nothing to add. That is what has happened here and I can tell you no more."

They seem to shrug. She has nothing to add and can say no more. Of course. Who would have thought otherwise? If she had something else to say, she would have said it. Wouldn't she? All of that seems reasonable.

Her long, thick pause, which in time dilation effect may be no more than a few seconds but then again may be several years (perhaps I am forcing this point, but it must be emphasized again and again that normal considerations of chronology just do not apply here), extends and then she says, "I was waiting now to hear from you."

They seem to look at one another. Perhaps an illusion of light. Then they look back at her.

"Well," she says, "well? You're all highly trained and qualified, not as qualified as John, perhaps, but surely amongst the three of you, you ought to be able to come up with something. I'm waiting. How do I get out of this?"

Still they say nothing. From the helpful, even eager aspect which can be seen glinting in the facade they present, it is obvious that they are not hostile, that they present no menace. They simply do not know what to do. Perhaps they make a few more shrugging gestures, if metal blocks can be said to shrug.

"Come on," Lena says.

They look as if they would be quite pleased to go on. But they say nothing.

"Well, look here, then," she says. "You can't just stay there. You must talk to me; I insist on it. You must have some good ideas."

"Well," one says and pauses, "well, then. The only means of escape would be to go directly into the tachyonic drive. To shift to faster-than-light speed without acceleration."

"That is true," another says. "Moving into faster-than-light speed without acceleration, that is. No tardyons, no gathering of force, but a clear shift."

"I've thought of that," Lena says. "The black hole contains all speeds below the speed of light, we can assume, since it is inhibiting light itself. But we don't know up to what limit it controls. It may contain even infinite speed."

"Nothing is infinite," one says. They really cannot be distinguished from one another. It would be nice to do those authorial things, neatly individuate the devices, even hint at a wisp of conflict between them, make them come alive through traits of character and argument, but how can this be done? You simply cannot make machines live, although the Bureau, in its reverence for its devices, has tried; and you cannot make machines different from one another except in technological specifications. No, there is nothing to be done; the situation must be accepted as it is. When one speaks, the others are quiet; when the three speak, they all sound the same. There is no difference. "Everything is finite," this one concludes.

"We don't know," she says; "nobody knows. That's why I've called on you."

Yet again they nod, slowly, bleakly. In truth their programs have not yet absorbed what she is talking about. They have only the dimmest grasp of the situation, but then again they have not had seventy thousand years to ponder the point. Even if they had had that amount of time, they function within a very slight range of cognition.

"Tardyons and tachyons, you see," Lena says. "Tardyons represent particles that move at less than the speed of light, tachyons those that move faster. Tardyons obviously won't work at all, not in terms of escape velocity here. I don't even know what state the craft is in at this point. I can't evaluate. I can't get a reading on any of this, although you can be sure that I've tried. Nothing about this is easy, you see."

"Tachyons," a cyborg says. "Yes, you are making that point clear. I can now understand what you are saying. It is difficult to grasp but it seems to make a certain sense." It confers with the others; they exchange information in little mumbles. If they were hooked up to the same computer bank, exchange would be immediate, but they are not, this being one of the Bureau's small economies. They cannot pool their information directly but must act in the halting fashion of humans.

"Unless you can think of something different," Lena says after they finish their discussion and have turned expectant blank cylinders to her once again. "Otherwise I'm going to be in here infinitely, and I just don't think that I can take much more of this really. Not with the dead."

"The dead? What about the dead?"

"You don't hear them?" Lena says. "You don't hear what's going on all the time?"

"I'm really afraid not," the cyborg assures her. It turns to the others. "Do you sense anything?" They make negative gestures. "What dead?" the cyborg says.

"Those in the hold."

"They would mean nothing. They are the dead and have no existence. Now I truly do not know what you are talking about."

"Here," she says, "here they have existence."

"I am afraid that you are wrong. The specifications are quite clear and you are misconceiving something."

"Perhaps I'm completely insane," Lena says quickly enough, "I've certainly had the opportunity to give that a lot of thought. That could very well be. It's a possibility anyway. Anyone could have been made crazy by this."

"Indeed."

"I've been in this field for seventy thousand years, and it's taken me almost all of this time simply to understand what's happening to us."

"Well," the same cyborg says, "ah, well." It seems to have assumed the role of speaker while the others stand by, rolling lightly in the motion of the ship which continues evenly as in a series of pulses which Lena can feel as pain to the depth of her senses but does not block thought. "Have you ever considered that it might be your destiny to *spend* infinity in this black hole."

"No."

"Maybe it is ordained in some fashion. Then again it may be inevitable. There might have been some cosmic disaster about which we know nothing but which has brought this on. In that case it would be impossible to get out. Anyway, the situation seems pretty hopeless as far as I'm concerned. Why don't you just relent? There seems to be a kind of immortality to it anyway, subjective immortality, of course, but what's the difference? It isn't everyone who could live seventy thousand years in any circumstances. Maybe you should just accept this fate."

"No," she says again. "No, I cannot. There is no cosmic accident. It is only *Skipstone* intercepting the field."

"Are you sure? Are you really sure of that? Perhaps you are in some way determining the condition, the force, the very *fate* of the universe."

"I don't understand."

"Don't you?"

"No," she says, "I don't. I don't know what you're talking about. Why does everything have to be concerned with the fate of the universe?" It is a cry not only from Lena, but also from the heart of the science fiction writer. "Why can't something just mean what it simply *means*? Why can't it be my own problem to suffer and to solve; why does it have to get tied in with the *universe*? Isn't my condition enough?"

"It was you who said that this might all be a gigantic accident," the cyborg points out. "Now didn't you say that? All existence might be an accidental by-product of the force of the implosion."

"I didn't know what I was saying," she says a little sulkily. "I'm not always responsible for everything that I say; everything doesn't have to *mean*—"

"Of course it does. Everything is related, you know that. Every act everywhere affects everything else, and perhaps your suffering here gives the universe purpose. Did you ever think of that?"

"No."

"Perhaps the implosion would not exist unless you were here to observe it. How can one tell about something like this? There are no easy answers. It is all very difficult and metaphysical."

"Metaphysical," the others say together, contrapuntally. "It is all metaphysical."

"At least you ought to consider it," the leader/spokesman says. "I wouldn't ignore anything that I'm saying here. Who can tell about something like this?"

"And then, too," the second cyborg/comforter says with just a slight lisp. (Possibly this is an individuating characteristic; in the absence of genuine inventive powers, one can always toss in a limp, a lisp, a cigarette, a stutter, a hint of bigotry. Look for these as the sign of an author or comic in trouble.) "If you say that the dead down there are alive—of course *we* can't hear a thing and you're probably quite mad, you know—but assuming that you're right and that they do have some kind of objective, external existence, well, then. What about that, I want to ask? Wouldn't that change the situation?"

"What situation?"

"Everything," the cyborg says rather grandly. "Nothing. The totality of it. You can't expect me to be specific about a matter like this; the conception is too grand to necessitate explanations. It just would be very important."

"I still don't understand," Lena says tensely. "I don't know what you're trying to tell me. I've come to you for answers and instead you're asking questions that are nonsense. Be practical. I'm trying to be; you could at least be the same."

Speaking at such length after seventy thousand years of subjective silence has made her weak. Cautiously she clears her throat, rasps, hawks, then spits. She runs a hand across her forehead, and it comes away glistening with sweat; she finds it amusing in a distant way that even here, in these circumstances, the ancient biological factors will nonetheless assert themselves. There is something important here. Even in a black hole one becomes weak, one sweats, one's throat tends to burn. An organism can become exposed to any kind of exotic parasites or bacteria but will always feel sick in a conventionally symptomatic fashion. His skin will not turn green nor will he be able to fly. The keyboard of human response is large but finite, and only certain harmonies can be played upon it no matter the impetus. Always, pain is referred back to the system; the system does not alter with the pain.

Abruptly she is filled with a revulsion so great that it becomes a palpable network which she feels glowing dimly within her. I should not have called upon them, she thinks, as if in the midst of illuminated wire, enfolding her, binding her inward, but then if I had not called upon them, what then? Would I have done it myself? What they are saying may be right. Possibly they have spoken nothing but the truth: that all of the universe swirls around this single pivot. If that is what has happened, then what am I to do? I do not know if I can manage a decision like this alone. I was not trained to make decisions; that was never the function for which the Bureau prepared us.

"I don't know about the deads," she says. "Maybe you're right about that; maybe I didn't hear them."

"Oh? Is that so?"

"I seem to have been in communication with one of them, but it may be an illusion. This could be. It is possible. I can accept and understand that I might be imagining them. But not entirely. And not the rest of it."

"But what if not?" the second says with a little urgency. "What if you do hear them? If somehow the black galaxy has brought them back to life, then an immediate vault into the tachyonic would destroy them for good."

I don't know. I can't tell about anything like that. Why can't you leave me alone?"

"It would be a lot of meat lost," the third rumbles in a rather self-important way. "One could say that about the dead. They are very valuable; they make possible all of the FTL experiments. If you were able somehow to return to Earth after this jolt, if it worked and you escaped the galaxy at whatever cost, I doubt very much if the Bureau would be congratulatory. It would be ruined cargo in that hold and they would be completely liable."

"So what?"

"So what? The estates would be litigious, the institutions which support the Bureau would be thrown into ruin. The legal complications alone would be enormous. It would be quite bad for you, Lena. You had better consider the dead, take them into account in all of your considerations here."

"I have been thinking of them."

"Not enough, then."

"I have, but I also have to think of *Skipstone* and of myself. Aren't *we* valuable?"

"Not so much."

"Don't I matter?"

"Not as much as the dead," the second says cheerfully; "not anywhere near them. If I were you, in fact, I think that I'd stay with them. Better to be lost and a mystery than to return and cause this kind of situation. Why, it would be the end of the project! Bureau would be unable to deal with this."

On his tiny conveyances the second, which has moved forward, moves back then against the bulkhead, much like an actor who has completed a monologue, and the others move in closer as if to confer with congratulatory murmurs. It is almost, Lena thinks, it is almost as if deep within their programs was implanted the need to preserve these dead at all costs, even from life which could take them only as a disease . . . but what else could she have expected? She knows the nature of this Bureau for which she works.

And as they do this, as she thinks that, a clamorous murmur seems to arise from the hold as if all of the dead were shrieking in exquisite pain, but whether this is coincidentally triggered or whether they have heard what the cyborg has said and this is their reaction is not known. And then, too, she might be imagining this. The cyborgs give no indication. How expressive can the dead be? How much can they tell? How much of this can be said to exist and what of it is dreams?

She listens and listens for that voice that has been in her mind for centuries . . . but she hears nothing, although her call beats against her chest like a bird, mingling with the lump of revulsion, binding, breaking and flowing then toward epiphany.

XXXII

To what degree can she disentangle from what she inhabits? This is part of her problem, and the other part is how much of what she inhabits has overtaken her so that she is no longer herself. She may have no more reality than the cyborgs. She may be a cyborg herself, of a more sophisticated type and without memory of how she was created; how otherwise could she have survived this? The originals would have the answer to this; so would the Bureau, but there is no way to make contact. What has been done to her? Are all of them here merely machines and the *Skipstone* a living being which contains them? Where is the line of demarcation between humanity and the machines?

"Well," the third cyborg says, not in response to this (the devices are certainly not telepathic), "well, I feel that I should make a statement here, *too.*" In a rather nervous gesture, absurd because these things are said not to feel, it twitches one of its cubes, revolves it slowly in position as it averts its line of sight from the omnipresent and dreadful portholes covered again. Do they really see, these things, or do they receive sensory impressions in a code which she could not understand? What is the quality of their consciousness, are they indeed conscious or merely feeding tape in a predetermined way for responses . . . and does it matter? Does any of this matter at all? For all the difference that it would make to her, they might see nothing.

"Ah, yes," the first says, "there is another point of view to be presented here that I think we should all attend to very closely."

"Right," the second lisps, "that's definitely right. There should be a whole range of points of view, after all. All articles of faith should be represented. What I am saying is right; it is the full and final truth of the matter, but I will be happy to know that other positions are represented and they should be, they should all be given their say. After all, this is an important decision here, very crucial."

"Crucial," the first whispers, "absolutely crucial. Everything is crucial and becoming increasingly so. Nothing will ever be trivial here."

"Indeed," the third says. It inclines its surfaces toward the second. "That has been stated very well, and as a matter of fact I couldn't have done it better myself. It really should be taken into consideration. I wanted to discuss what could be called the more cosmic implications of what is going on here."

"You should," the first says, "and so you very definitely should. I'm glad that you had the courage to bring it up. That shows very rare courage."

"Right," the third says and then to Lena: "Now listen here. Listen to me and attend this. You've fallen into a neutron star, a black funnel. It's utterly beyond your puny capacities to escape it, and the dimensions of what has happened here would reduce you to inconsequence. What can be done against forces like these? You've got to submit, got to accept the situation."

"I don't want to believe that," Lena says.

"You had better."

"Man can overcome anything. He can voyage anywhere."

"But he cannot voyage out."

"What he sees, he understands; what he understands, he can master. Nothing is beyond us."

"That's puerile thinking."

"No, it isn't."

"Certainly it is. It's the same puerility which put you here to begin with, and you still don't seem willing to accept the truth. Can the dead overcome death?"

"They have."

"*They have not.* It is all in your imagination. There are places man was not meant to go, objects he was not meant to touch, emotions beyond his ability to interpret, and this is all of them. You must yield. You must face the futility of the situation. I would recommend that you look for a religious solution. That would probably serve you better than anything at this time."

"He's quite right," the second adds. "That's a very good point that's just been made up here. Surrendering, absolutely yielding control of the situation, is *always* a reasonable option, and here it's been forced upon you. It would be stupid not to interpret the signals, wouldn't it? After all, you'd just be doing what you've been told."

"That's easy for you to say," Lena says. She is responding blindly now, no longer thinking, merely continuing the disputation by reflex as it were. "After all, you're just machines. You aren't even that; you're a series of tapes and memories. How could you suffer as I am? Furthermore, you don't have my responsibilities. You won't be the ones to have to deal with the Bureau; I will. You won't be held responsible for this at all."

"Now how do you know?" the third says reasonably. "How can you make an easy statement like that? Can you judge the suffering of machines? Have you ever been one? Part of all of us was once human so that we can make some comparison, but have you ever been a machine? Now think of *that.*"

"Maybe I'm a machine now and I'm dreaming all of this. Maybe this is another simulation."

"Don't be ridiculous," the first says snappishly. "Just face the realities here and give up. It's been the only real option that has been presented to you from the start of this hopeless situation: to give up and accept your fate. If I were in your position, I would. You're just being stubborn."

"The Bureau will understand," the second lisps. "Believe me, they'd appreciate what you're up against here. They'd approve of this and they'd be proud of you for doing what was best to protect *their* interests."

"The Bureau never gave up," Lena says. "The Bureau sent me out here. If it weren't for them, this wouldn't have happened to begin with, just remember that. It's their responsibility, not mine. Anything that I do, I'm doing for them as much as for myself, and they'll know it."

"But it's too late now anyway," the third says. "That's just sophistry, and that kind of thing doesn't work these days. These are modern times, hard-boiled, practical, you've got to come to terms with the way things are and deal with them as they are. This is no time for idealism or whining around. As you know I used to be a physicist; I was originally made part of the equipment so that I would be able to advise you on any emergencies that had a physical science basis. I'm the expert in that area, and you have to take my word on anything that is said, and I've had plenty of opportunity now to calculate what's happened here. If I were you, I'd accept it. I'd just give up and let the ship fall and try to make the best of what is admittedly a very bad situation. The other way lies madness and futility, and you don't want to pursue that."

"I'm already mad."

"No, you're not. Not if you've been able to make presentation the way you have."

"That's nonsense."

"But, Lena, you are brilliantly, totally sane! Your mental facilities are absolutely intact. Despite the chaos here, there is not a sign of schizoid break."

"I'm suffering," she says. Her voice takes on inflection for the first time during this. "I'm suffering terribly. The dead are suffering also; I've taken on their condition, I share it with them now. There's at least a theoretical possibility that we can get free of this."

"How? Not at all."

"I exit without acceleration."

"Utterly destructive."

"Switch directly to tachyonic drive. Move immediately beyond light speed."

"There's no precedent for that, Lena. It's never been heard of; it goes counter to all the established rules of physical motion. Even if it isn't theoretically impossible, which it may well be, but even if it weren't, you can't do that. You cannot gauge the effects."

"This is a situation unlike any before. It demands new and special measures. How can we know what we can do until we've faced doing it? How can we say what our limits are until we've gone beyond to test them?"

"You're talking nonsense, Lena. Vainglorious nonsense which does not befit you."

"And then, too," the first says, "what if you do attempt this hasty and disastrous course, this selfish and stupid blunder? Where will you emerge?"

She has thought of that. She has given it a good deal of consideration, more than she would want to concede to the comforters. "I don't know," she says.

"You could land in the heart of a star. You could land at an edge of the universe where at no speed could you ever return.

You might come embalmed in rock on some planet. You might put *Skipstone* into explosion."

"I know that."

"You might destroy the foundations of the cosmos. The destabilization might be that profound. Have you thought of what might happen if you land in another neutron star?"

"Yes."

"You argue that all rules of space and time have been destroyed here and that only gravity persists. But would the fall not end eventually? There must be finite limits; at some point you will be drawn into the black hole and come out the other end of it into some other universe or some part of this one."

"No," she says, "I've thought about that. It took me a long time to work that one through, but if the very shape of space is changed by the gravitational field, then the fall would be infinite. It would have to be. There would be no point of termination, because we are falling inside curved space, a null space which lacks any of the properties which we can associate—"

"All right," the physicist cyborg says, cutting her off as if disturbed. "You've had a chance to evaluate and come to that explanation. You may be right, although I disagree, but we won't argue that at this time; we'll defer to the thought you've given. It doesn't matter. The point still is, where will you come out if you break free?"

"And I told you," she says, "I told you that already. I don't know. I have no idea."

"In truth there's no way to calculate it, is there? It just becomes chance; the coordinates are beyond computation and you could be anywhere at all."

"That's possible."

"You had better think of that. If I were you, I would have given that serious thought."

"I have."

"And what then?"

"Anything would be better than this, that's what I think. This can't go on."

"Why can't it?"

"Because it's unbearable."

"You cannot gauge where you would show up, you fool. Can't you understand the scope of the universe? You're heading into infinite possibilities of which all human life occupies the tiniest sector. Your coordinates are antihuman and antilife."

"What do you care?"

"We care about the fate of the universe. You might unbalance the cosmos. A sudden matter transfer. There is no way of gauging these things, Lena. There is no way in which the shifts could be anticipated. The dropping of mass—"

"Oh, go to hell," she says furiously." Damn it, go to hell. You're supposed to help me here, not fight. You were put here so that I could call on you, so that I wouldn't have to fight this alone, and what have you done? What has happened to me? All you want to do is to do things to convenience the Bureau. That's all the Bureau cares about."

"It cares about not destroying the universe."

"Why does everything have to do with the destruction of the universe?" she says again. "Can't you just deal with people, can't you understand that there are *people* here? I matter; I matter more than the Bureau does."

"You know you really don't mean that."

"I do mean it. I didn't activate you for you to tell me what not to do or how impractical I was. I wanted you to go over the thinking with me and tell me that I was right."

"But you're not right," the third says. "Your thinking is entirely wrong."

"I'm the captain!"

"You are not in a command position. You are merely another piece of equipment on *Skipstone* responsible for the maintenance of the other equipment. You are the servant of the ship, not its master, and you are," the third says with a sigh which has personality, it is as if the full burden of humanity had come upon it if only for an instant, certain tapes activated which thrust upon it the mannerisms of the person it had been, "you are to remain here," it says, "and maintain the ship in a standby alert position. You are to do nothing to try to leave the field. It is unfortunate that this has happened, but it was a chance that you took when you assumed the responsibility, and you can't get out of it now."

"I am not," Lena says, "I am not going to stay here. I am going to do exactly what I want"

"You are willful."

"I don't care. I don't care what I am. I'm going to do this no matter what you say. I'm going to gear the ship up to tachyonic drive and try to get all of us out of here."

"No," the second says, similarly inflected. It is remarkable how the context of the discussion has changed; now it is Lena who is calm, the cyborgs who are screaming. "No, I really wouldn't want to do that. You and the dead are joined together now. It is a shared fate and was always meant to be this way. You must remain with them. You are part of the dead."

"No, I am not."

"Ah, well," the first cyborg says. "You have to consider the mysteries here. What is life? What is death? What is the difference between the two, where do they meet and where does the division begin? Consider these questions."

"That's a good point, Lena. Those are good questions. I really would."

"Impenetrable mysteries."

"Darkness, theology."

"You can penetrate the very core of existence with this, Lena. Life and death existing together in this fall. Think of it: the symbolic fall heightening the symbolism here if you want to pursue it. Why it's fascinating! You may be able to work out the full and final answers here."

"An exquisite opportunity."

"Exquisite, I'd say."

"Remarkable. Wholly remarkable. You will be able to glimpse, as no other human ever has, the eternal and the essential."

"You will never regret this, Lena."

"We'll stay with you, if you desire. We'll render you all the companionship you could need."

"Oh, definitely. Definitely. Well give you a great deal of support."

"We can share this. Together."

"I wouldn't pass this up if I were you, Lena. It's never been offered anyone before."

"Oh, no. Never."

"Never again, either. What a small price to pay for understanding! It's remarkable."

"No," she says again, dazzled by the comforts, their interchangeability in dialogue, their persuasiveness, their solidity of purpose now that they seem finally to have accepted her own seriousness. But she knows, too, that the historical and theological role of comforters has always been to mislead (and if she does not know it then the author, busily straining over the levers of the plot in the cockpit of his own attention certainly does), and she will not be dissuaded. "No, I will not listen to you. There are no solutions. You offer me no solutions at all."

"We do. We—"

"There are only mysteries," she says, "and they can never be solved, but we can cultivate a decent respect for them and try to deal with them in relation to the mystery of our own humanity," and then she turns from them, breaking their hold upon her with a mere suspension of attention, goes to the place where the thing that was John lies, crouches over it like an animal and just for a little while she weeps. For herself, for him, for the lies, for the flight. For the dead in space. For the failure of her own belief that the Bureau, at one time, must have cared for her.

XXXIII

But shortly she feels better and the time is done for weeping. Furthermore, she knows that what has been discharged is more profound than tears; it is a whole level of feeling which she will never have again and without which, like a swimmer, she will be able to move more swiftly through the dark waters of purpose. The conversation has discommoded her as the Bureau intended the comforters to do, but it has also brought her to a new level; now, past disorientation and the shaken poles of faith, she begins to sense a new order. She must depend wholly upon herself. In one sense it is posited that this dialogue is taking place in a ship falling madly in a quality of space which could never be described, but in another it can be seen as one of those elegant and terrible drawing-room exchanges so popular with the discredited practitioners of the well-made play in which the slightest alteration of point of view or opinion is supposed to create great tension.

Any tension, however, is that generated between the furnaces of the dying star, ten million explosions a minute, and *Skipstone*, arc in its heavens. Lena, knowing this, feels numb. Having moved beyond the comforters, she feels that she has learned little, and yet she must persist. She cannot turn over the very little she has learned to the iron hearts of the machines.

"Fuck you," she says.

They say nothing. Scatology does not move them any more than reason. If anything, their efforts have drained them and left them without visible effect. They lurk like crouched animals, only the slight whirring of their transistors indicating that they are still functional.

"Fuck you all," she says again. "I'm going to do it and I always was from the beginning. I'm going to get us out of here. It's all a plot of the Bureau, anyway, to prevent me from getting back should I run into some disaster. I'll come out all right; I don't care what you told me. It's all lies. Bureau just doesn't want the embarrassment of my returning to tell the tales. They don't want anyone to know what's going on in space, what it's really like. They were plotting this from the beginning; they just want a smooth path so that they can conquer the world. They don't give a damn about the universe." She realizes that, although she has phrased this crudely, she probably believes it, that she has always believed it. She puts her hands near the console. All along she hated those in the Bureau. She should have known. If she had only touched her feelings, she would have known the nature of that with which she was dealing. "I'm going to turn you off now," she says. "You'll never know the difference anyway when we escape. You'll be dismantled when we get back, so you'll never know a thing. What do you care? It's going to be much easier for you than for me; I'm going to have to go through."

The first says, almost agreeably, "You're right. We have no instinct of self-preservation."

"Indeed," the second says with similar amiability. "I'm finding this quite wearying, and I never did have a forceful personality, even at the best."

"If we had self-preservative instincts, it would be too diffi-cult and painful," the first says cheerfully. "Fortunately, we're willing to be deactivated. As far as we're concerned, we did our absolute best. The problem is not ours now."

"Me, too," says the third. "I can go along with that completely. I mean, just because we have an argument here, because we tell you a few things that we were programmed to say, don't think that we don't have any feelings, because we do, or at least if we did, we'd feel very badly about this. We're just trying to do what we can in your own best interests, that's all."

"Liars," Lena says. "Now you're trying to win my confidence and get me to go along with you by pretending to agree. I don't believe anything that you're saying. You'll never make me believe it, no matter what you do. I won't cooperate with any of your schemes; I see through you."

"But it's true," the first says, "all true. You don't have to get paranoid about this just because we've lost an argument and are willing to admit it. You know, you're entitled to do what you want to; it's your decision. Stay here or, if you wish, leave. Of course it would be much nobler of you, in probability, to remain here. For all we know your condition gives substance and vitality to the universe. Maybe the basic stresses here are those from which all existence itself came to begin with and you are now at the beginning of time. How do you like that? Good irony, no, and certainly of a large scale! But if time is suspended, *you* may have caused the universe, Lena, you and *Skipstone*. You and the ship have generated everything. From your acci-dent came everything including those very conditions which led to the accident. Hah!"

"Madness," Lena says, shaking her head, "that's utter madness," but the author, busily pulling the handles of his little dumb show, sweating behind the canvas, casting a nearsighted, astigmatic eye every now and then through the cardboard of the set to see whether the audience is paying attention, how the audience is taking all of this, is thinking take *that* Barth, Barthelme, Roth or Oates! *Pace* Bellow and Malamud, and may your Guggenheims multiply, but what have any of you or those unnamed created to compare with this? *Angst*, this is the sigh from which all self-pity once must have come. But the author ducks away, keeps his mind on business, modestly looks away from the audience and then down, transmuting (as he tries to except at very weary moments) his responses, histories, revulsion or envy to his characters. That is, after all, the more lasting and satisfying way to do this. "That would be insane," Lena says; "it would reduce all circumstance, *all* of it, to a circular accident caused by that accident. It would mean that there was no purpose in anything other than to create purposes and that—"

"But why not? What other reason would be as sufficient? You might have created the universe, you might even *be* the universe, come to think of it, but," the first concludes, "you aren't going to listen to any of this so I won't argue the point. We agreed to end disputation; it won't get us anywhere. You win, we lose. You'll have to handle this your way."

"Not so. I want to *save* the mission. I want; don't you understand that I want to return the dead—"

"Rationalization, Lena. Shut off the console now. Shut it off, deactivate us."

"All right," she says, "all right then, I will. You want me to do that—"

"*You* want to do it, Lena. You'll be much happier then and so will we. What do you care if you deny all existence by following this course? But we won't argue the point further. We really won't. It's in your hands, it always was, we were never anything more than abstractions anyway," the first concludes rather mysteriously and then makes a gesture to the other two, something sly and secret in the glint, some level of communication between cyborgs that Lena could not enter, would not understand if she could. In tandem they roll solemnly to the porthole like children trundling their awkward way across a floor. "We'll just have ourselves a good look at this," the cyborg says; "we'll have a look at this so-called black galaxy that you've warned us about."

"Don't," Lena says, "now please don't do that. There's no need, no need at all—"

"Of course we will," says the second.

"You bet your life we will," the third says.

"We're absolutely unanimous on this point," says the spokesman; "you can see that if it's going to be done your way then it has to be done ours as well," and the first thrusts aside the curtain again, poking its cylindrical snout, and Lena has an idea. She will get to the console and deactivate the cyborgs manually before they can do what they are seeking, but she does not have enough time to do so. In mid-lunge she is cut off, and then the pure, spectral range of the black galaxy pours through.

She shrieks, covers her eyes, fights with the switches and so at last, by accident, hits the lever of cancellation, shutting off the power in the cyborgs, and they collapse then in sequence by the porthole, curtains swinging closed, lying there in metallic disarray, clutching one another in a human and dependent fashion as if the moment of confrontation had driven them out of metal and wire and made them human again, made them seek one another. Lena begins, not unemotionally, to weep. It is manufactured sheerly by emotion and pity; there is nothing else to it.

But her weeping will pass, everything will pass, there are only certain limits past which emotional anguish can be carried before the psyche seals off, the reflexes of pain are numbed and the reader, too, loses belief, and so in time, kicking the machines aside so that they need not distract her anymore, Lena returns to the business at hand which is now clear to her. She knows what she must do.

She must will herself to the controls and begin the dance of the tachyons. She must concentrate on dangerous eviction that might destroy all.

XXXIV

So this can be said: that the novel sits upon a predetermined conclusion. She will attempt to flee the hold of the neutron star; she either will or will not succeed. Whatever that outcome, the penultimate decision is highly visible, and the textual material interposed between the statement of the problem and that solution is merely a lever for delay. It is quite clear what is going to happen; it is merely a matter of springing that conclusion, and in this sense the novel is not unlike traditional classic tragedy or its modern descendants such as *Death of a Salesman* or *Marat/Sade*, where suspense is not predicated so much upon what will happen to the principals as to how many mutually enriching levels of narrative irony can precede that end.

It should be clear by now, then, that the denouement of this novel has been obvious from the presentation of the problem. Lena, against all urgings and reasonable possibility, will essay to leave the hold of the neutron star through that power which *Skipstone* can give her. The reader, knowing this, may become restive, may have been running out of patience for some chapters before this. Why not get on with it? he might ask. Why not have her make the attempt, win or lose, wrap it up, but get out of this? What is being gained by holding back on discovery?

But to say this is to miss the point. I do not wish to accuse the reader; this is the simple basis of the matter. This novel is not about what happens to her—which is merely a function of astronomies after all—but why it has happened and what real effects this must have upon everyone, including the reader. The *whyness* of matters. The question not of consequence but of implication.

XXXV

So it is clear that the satiric aspects of the scene with the comforters could have been milked for great and widening implication, and unless a skillful and controlling hand were kept upon the material, the novel could, at this point, be well on the way toward the truly farcical.

Consider this. Here is, after all, a background woven of the metaphysical and the hard sciences on a canvas of the inconceivably vast, yet before this construction is being enacted hastily and with a tint of the disreputable the same old comedy, the same folly, the same easy and dreadful juxtapositions of character which would fuel the dullest of well-made plays. Has the novel voyaged out to such inconceivable destination merely to bring the same old messages of human spite and mechanical pointlessness? Is this going to be a recapitulation of the same wearying human limitations which could occur in any split-level beside the intersection of the new interstate with Old Armonk Road, rubber toys in the small backyard, the crabgrass glinting under the haze of the suburban moon? This would be a legitimate question; it will not easily be defeated. The material would indeed have to be handled carefully and with an awareness of how easily it might descend to the riotous. Pain would have to be wrenched out of it; the reader would have to feel with the characters. Not only intellectual content but levels of the ambiguous would have to be woven through less *Galaxies* become merely an attack upon the technological, a curse against that absurdity. Nothing, surely, could be further from the intent of the novel. Yet the danger is there. Let it be acknowledged.

Even as the least talented comedian working in the dullest and dirtiest nightclub in the outskirts of Jamaica, Queens, New York, would know, great issues can be reduced to the scatological simply by particularization, by bringing them to the level of common, human necessity. Napoleon had to move his bowels; Hitler had itches; the Kennedys believed in Camelot and said prayers before bedtime (certain biographers informed us) but also had moments of false climax and sieges of pus. The sad stories of the death of kings might have had to do with constipation or embarrassing hemorrhage; the royal families of several nations have had a hereditary syphilis. Similarly, the novel must risk trivialization by bringing its material to the level of human necessity, and the scene with the cyborg, with its clanking, its religious (or antireligious) satire and even the whiff of a fart here or there, cosmological farts to be sure, might well furnish needed comic relief to what is, after all, a rather depressing construct.

In fact, in fact: why fight the issue? It would be best to accept and utilize the humor that can be found in various passages; to take one's relief where one can get it. There is no reason why the novel has to be negative; to the contrary. If it can find humor in *this*, the unstated message might be, well, then, it can find humor in anything. Matters cannot be quite that bad after all.

(Then, too, it could be easy to wring from the material the fact that, even surrounded by the cosmos and the palpable edge of the universe, man remains a corrupt and flatulent race; the fart will outweigh the metaphysical cry anytime at all. One remains what one must be regardless of circumstance. Could the reader settle for this and let the novel go there?)

But, of course, there is ample material available to save from itself this scene with the cyborgs, to keep the novel on track and to make sure that at no point does the construction depart from its basic vision.

And that basic vision must be nothing less than the setting of the final chapters.

XXXVI

For it must be lush in physical depiction of the black galaxy, of the neutron star, of the altering effects that each will have had upon the perceived reality. There must be a heightened sense of the visual; surely it is this otherness which must be communicated, and therefore descriptive passages will not be scanted. Indeed, every time the plot seems to flag, when the dialogue becomes flat, the characters hysterical or the author unctuous, at every such point when the narrative drive appears to falter, *Galaxies* will drag itself over to the portholes to deep and wondering looks at the terrain of exploration.

And here is the source of the ultimate power, that which will excuse it from the many deficiencies inevitable with such a scheme. For the terrain is one which can be offered only in the broadest and most ambitious of science fiction, and every rhetorical trick, every typographical device, every nuance of language and memory which the author has in his scruffy, dusty bag of techniques sitting by the typewriter will be called upon to describe the appearance of the galaxy, the effects that the galaxy has upon all those who enter it. Lena—who one must admit is a rather superficial character; there just is not all that much to her, although she is not devoid of sympathetic traits—will nonetheless be used to the limit of her expressive possibilities to work this through; nor will the writer, aware of another factor here, dismiss the dead, who also feel in this space and who can communicate this response.

Needless to say, this will be a rather bleak vision. There is no way to avoid that; the novel can hardly be said to be optimistic, for the effect the galaxy will have upon anyone trapped will be quite terrible. It results in a complete alteration of consciousness, and the hold which most of us have upon our vision of reality, our assessment of life, is already sufficiently tentative to make almost anything attacking it quite threatening. But with all of that bleakness, with all of the lush and rather prurient imagery which will be used to show how the effects act to destroy consciousness, the novel will not be completely hopeless. Not at all. In fact it will be possible for some to say (and some may even say it) that rather than being terrible the vision is somehow "poetic" here or "optimistic."

For, if the rhetorical effects are properly applied, if the writing shows power and control, then the construct will demonstrate, finally, that those concepts which we label "beauty" or "ugliness" or "good" or "evil" or "love" or "life" or "death" are little more than metaphors, poorly ascribed, semantically limited, refracted through the weak receptors which we possess to the utter diminution of what they really mean, and it will be suggested that, rather than showing us an alternate reality, the black galaxy may only be showing us our own but *extended*, opened up so that the novel may give us, as science fiction can in the rare times when it is good and as almost nothing else ever can, some glimpse of possibilities beyond ourselves, possibilities not truly compensated by word rates or the problems of categorization to a limited audience.

What is love? What is death? What is the meaning of all this anyway? The author does not want to start metaphysical disquisition at this or any other point. Sections of an author's novels written in his true voice are always the dullest and least affecting; the philosophical opinions of writers are of no use to anyone, the writers least of all. The good novelists can compose novels, all right, but even the best of them cannot think, and the "opinions" of a writer taken out of the mask of characterization or structure are always as banal as those of politicians. The ability to create character or assemble a set of narrative materials does not qualify the opinions of the author. If anything, they must be more suspect than those of an essayist: who, after all, is doing the talking? In what persona is the writer speaking now? So the reader will be spared, not only in this set of working notes, but also in the novel itself, laborious and mystical ramblings on the nature of things like "love" or "death" or "theme" or "religion" or "ultimate significances."

Who cares? Tolstoy went crazy, Mailer ran for mayor, Dos Passos looked for Communists, Sinclair Lewis went foursquare for Main Street, Kerouac ended hating children. Something happens to writers past the point of their creative options, something obscene, like the damages (not only of age) on the faces of prostitutes or the aspect of actors lumbering their way through retirement homes for grand old troupers. Considering that the best of them will end as fools, the best that a writer can do, it would seem, would be to cultivate a decent silence which will at least hold his folly to himself, and there are a few contemporary examples of this approach, which are worth emulating.

The reader, in any case, need not be concerned by this. The writer's silence is not immediate but will have to do only with the longer range; if the writer is to become silent, he will not do it in the midst of this novel which deserves a smashing climax and which will receive it. There is time, there is time: there is the rest of the writer's life, after all, in which to cultivate silence, and for the time being his obligations are clear: to follow smoothly if discursively through all of the issues raised here to an ending which will not deprive the reader of his expectation that there is some order and that the reeds of this narrative will not blow their way into silence, discord and white noise to conclude the wry and tentative harmonies suggested.

XXXVII

Interwoven as well will be the more human story of Lena's containment and suffering. She will, thus, be a "warm" and "sympathetic" character most identifiable to the reader so that he will be able to participate more fully in the abstract sections of the story. She will lead him there.

If Lena failed to come alive, if the reader could not feel sympathy for her plight and respond in a way which will enable him to find the outcome personally involving, this would be a cold, distant performance, brilliance in the way that the technically efficient can be, of course, but devoid of those qualities of pain which are worth more than technical briskness. "Pain" or "warmth" are by certain standards reserved to the catalog of merely commercial or sentimental literature, but if these qualities are not incorporated here, this novel will lose intrinsic value.

So characteriological touches for Lena will not be skimped. Consider her as she comes struggling to individuation: the reader should see her as an admirable person for all her faults, really remarkably courageous in the face of all her disasters, her seventy thousand years, her one thousand lives. Her own character emerges from all of them; her determination to seek and remain herself is touching. Throughout all of it she has held on to her own character and her goal and this is not unremarkable.

This accretion of sympathy can be managed through a bag of fictional techniques, some of them conventional, some more ambitious. Individuation through defining idiosyncrasy, for instance: tricks of speech, habits, mannerisms and so on. The kind of thing which could have been applied to the scene with the cyborgs if the writer had not had such an excess of integrity. Stammer or lisp, hitch in pace, a sudden characteristic stumble or aversion to odors as she limps across the cabin to check the portholes. Rhetorical devices peculiar to her, as in the instances of sex with John where her rhetoric becomes florid. Little physical signs, a large bosom or cast in the eye if nothing of greater originality occurs. Keep those devices modest and visible, however; science fiction is bizarre enough without increasing the distance of characters from the reader.

Any competent writer knows how to do this. So do the incompetent ones, sometimes better, which blurs distinctions further. But competent or incompetent, we all pretty much know what to do: set off one character against all the others in a scene by something visible, or at any rate easily grasped, so that the reader will be able to make mental pictures, hear distinct sounds. Feel that the character is a recognizable human being just as himself. The reader, that only true participant, that only character in a novel the reader himself must invent with only the code of language to help him on his way, needs all of the suggestions he can get. Individuation is not to be mocked nor is this to be scorned. Without it fiction is merely shadow play, disembodied ideas struggling through the haze, some glimpse of ruined forms gasping their way through the wasteland which is already of our time and which the reader has pursued fiction to avoid.

(Even with the cunning use of these devices, it is a miracle that fiction exists at all. Consider the code, consider the network, the levels of abstraction. Even a bad writer, an uneasy reader, is a kind of miracle. In writing or reading alike, one must completely reconstruct that which does not exist at all without participation.)

Still, science fiction, that glittering literature of ideas or at least pseudo ideas, poses particular problems for all of us. In common, everyday fiction, the kind which our academic or *Redbook* writers alike write so bravely, we could give Lena her affecting stutter, dimple on the left breast, tremor in the right cheekbone, love of old houses, hatred of old houses, hatred of dimples, love of stutter, fear of noise, acceptance of flight, twitch of finger under stress and go no further. From these encoded signals, all would be able to infer their own state of mind. But in this difficult and highly abstract novel, because of the abstract nature of the theme, the way that the theme floods the very characterization and, in fact, can be said to overtake it, it will be necessary to do more than slash clumsy ribbons of paint at the archetypes on the shelf. One will have to find originalities of idiosyncrasy which in their suggestivity will approximate the black hole itself. If the situation, that is to say, is really crazy, then Lena will have to be really crazy, too, in order to convey it. Otherwise all will come off as grotesquerie instead of as a sharpened, careful assault upon the conditions which squeeze life into their shape rather than submitting to it. This will not be easy. It will tax the modest powers of invention available to me.

"I'm crazy," Lena might say staring through her hands, observing that fine translucence through which she can see the network of the ship itself, fine streaks of wire running through the metal like cobwebs, "I'm crazy; I would have to be crazy to remain here, even to be alive through all of this." The engines still maintaining the support systems give a confirmatory throb. "I've got to be mad," she says; "how else could this be?" She stumbles away, feeling her body extended to infinite dimensions, feeling herself as an extension that can overtake any part of the ship. Bigger than the black galaxy itself, she sends her persona to invade all of *Skipstone*, plants a betraying, informative kiss upon the dead in the hold. "Take that," she says, "take that if you think you're out of it. You fall deeper and deeper as do I; life and death have no meaning here. Do you see where all your dreams have gotten you, where your mad wills and inheritances have taken? You wanted to live again, and so you are, and, therefore, if I were you, I would choose death, but it's too late, too late for any of that now. You'll just have to take it as it is and make the best of it. You're crazy, too," she might point out to the dead; "all of us are here, otherwise we could not possibly survive this."

A legitimate technique, this, turning the substance of the novel against what has seemed its first tension. Lena is not trying to remain sane but to be mad as efficaciously as possible, and the ironies here are workable. But enough, enough of that: the problems of the writer are not those of the reader. Even as the writer struggles to invent a novel, he must somehow entertain and induce that efficient briskness which is the key to diversion, particularly in so-called escape literature. The reader is not concerned with the author's fatigue, his almost constant series of complaints, his persistent horror of the act of writing, his domestic problems, car problems, financial problems, gray obsessions, light obsessions, slashes and dashes and smashes of fatigue which in the midst of his best efforts suddenly make him feel trivial and old. No, none of these factors can interest the reader whose attention through these complaints has already started to break up like patches of ice under sun. Soon it will vanish into little clots of damp, drying to bone. Why *this* book? the reader asks himself, now well into the fourth hour of his continental flight, staring through little clouds, a child's vision of heaven, toward a wing, wondering exactly when fire will burst from that wing and he will see his death sketched out against the sky, turning away from the window to look past sleeping businessmen and a fat woman knitting furious epitaphs between her hands, looking for a stewardess—more asepsis— with whom he can establish some contact. Why did I buy this one? the earnest and suffering reader wonders; why didn't I pick something to the left and right? *Staggers of the Slime Planet* had a cover almost as attractive. Do I really want or need this? the reader thinks, shaking his head and moving his agonized shoulder blades several inches to and fro in a rabbit's gesture, trying to work out the stiffness and itching from the core of his back. Why did I take this flight? Couldn't I have taken one at night? Do I really have to see this person, these people in Los Angeles? Couldn't it have been let go for another six months? What is there to gain at this moment from reconciliation and why didn't I order the second complimentary Gibson, when several days ago the stewardess asked me if I would like it?

No, this will get me nowhere, the reader thinks; I am descending into futility; I must be positive-minded and forward-looking. *Galaxies* is confusing, but here are elements of tension, there are certain mind-broadening concepts, over here in the corner is the promise of a flaming and dramatic resolution; if I can hold on through all of this, I have enough faith in the author to know that I will not be cheated.

Still, he thinks, turning petulant and self-pitying the way that most of us do and no harm in it, self-pity being virtually the only emotion with which a sane person can confront life, still it is not fair. Here is a novel which seems to lurch in and out of its textual material like a drunk trying to find a line on the sidewalk or a jockey looking for an opening along the rail; it cannot possibly transport me from the more ominous and terrifying perspectives to be gained from looking at the wing tip. Where are all those college girls and divorcees? Where are those women with whom one is supposed to be able to establish contact during long flights or bus trips? Surely this cannot be my destiny entire. There has got to be more to this than there seems to be.

The writer has sympathy. Indeed, I can understand the problem here, can only assure in return that none of this is self-indulgent, that *Galaxies* tracks its purposes as relentlessly as the breathing of the reader's seatmates tracks and holds the beat of the jets in the nostrils. Bear with me and find not only resolution, but also excitement and adventure to exceed even what has gone heretofore. Science fiction is an adventurous format. Science fiction is a medium of wonder.

Lena will be individuated and thus become far more accessible. Her individuation will be accomplished in sections which will be interwoven with the more objective if surreal descriptions of the properties of the black galaxy. Although this meshing of personality and astrophysics will be dazzling and even verge upon tour de force, it will, in truth, be the easiest technical problem of the novel to solve. Two skills which fall well within my range—flat, deadpan, descriptive prose and highly charged sexual imagery—will effortlessly complement one another, giving an impression of more depth than may even be present. Technique can often supplant reason. Sometimes it may become meaning itself.

XXXVIII

But let it be made clear again; this is not a novel but merely a set of notes for one. The novel itself remains unutterably beyond our time and hence outside of the devices of fiction. It moves beyond any considerations of normal space, can be glimpsed only in those empty little flickers of light which reveal the galaxies much as Lena cannot see the neutron star but only sense its effects, much as Lena can only infer the gravity, not gauge it. These notes are surely as close to the narrative as anyone of this time can get, because the novel cannot be written for almost two thousand years . . . but let us not become megalomaniacal in the pursuit of theme. These are merely notes. They are not definitive. The very language of the techniques necessary to write it will not be ours for two millennia.

Still, one does the best that one can under the situation presented. Little more can be asked of a writer. There will be long descriptive sections idiosyncratizing Lena and making her visible to the reader. She will talk to him by talking to herself; she will laugh, cry, mourn, express wonder at the dimensions of her situation, know moments of terror. She may (but then again she may not; we will see, it will be my decision) engage in streams of consciousness triggering flashbacks which will lend characterizational veracity. We will know more than what is necessary in order to accept her reality.

As these sections end, they will draw upon the conclusion that Lena has made her decision to leave the black galaxy by the dangerous means which are her only option. She will try to convert to FTL drive without acceleration. This decision has squirmed through her preconscious (not the author's; he has no opinion on the subject) and now is in the front of that part of her brain responsible for making rational evaluation. She does not know where she will emerge or when, just as the comforters have warned her, but she does know that this must be the way in which *Skipstone*'s tragedy and her own must end.

She prepares to set the controls for the plunge, her breath shallow and moist within her but laid against the rasp and controlled rhythm of her purpose. She knows that what she is doing is best for all of them here.

But before she can do it, she must tell them. She must tell those who will be most affected by this. She must make sure that they understand the situation and share her approach, that they accept the inevitability as she has.

She locks the controls, musing, and sets off to make confrontation with the dead.

XXXIX

For in a sense the dead have controlled everything; they are not the mere cargo but the creation of the voyage. If it were not for their presence, their generosity, their estates, their greed and terror, the FTL experiments would not have been at all financially feasible; if it were not for the lives transmuted now by the effects of the black galaxy to impinge upon Lena's consciousness, she might not be sentient at all. She might have died in the subjective time imposed by the gravity. It is only the cargo, then, that has kept her shielded against what would have otherwise been utter fragmentation; by using first one personality and then the next, the thousand, as interposition against the forces of the fall, she would have disintegrated. She knows this and knows that there has been a conscious element of use.

But she knows something else as well which is even more significant: the FTL experiments, Lena has come to understand (and with her the writer himself), the FTL experiments have always been shaped by the dead; in truth they fed upon the quality of death, and the Bureau, consciously or not, has shaped itself utterly around that cargo. There must have been some irony in that position, an irony that was built deeply into the projects, and that irony would be this: what was supposedly life-enforcing and expanding was sustained only by the presence of death. From the very beginning the experiments, rather than using the dead, have been their celebration. They have exalted it. That was what was really going on here from the start.

In the black galaxy, life and death have intermingled. But this is merely an extension, a concrete physical manifestation of what has been true from the beginning. Without the dead there is no life. Life has embraced the dead. All together they fall, and the gravitation is their mortality, plunging them relentlessly toward the sun that will fold them through to another way of life.

XL

Leaning over the console, then, she permits one of the dead to come forth and address her, no expectation in her bearing, merely the willingness to allow, finally, the dead to overtake her. What she does is without thought or even conscious intention, merely the extension of necessity.

She need make no formal gesture to summon the dead. They have been battering on her skull, screaming for seventy thousand years, and now, with a single, mental whisk, she has merely permitted all of those partitions to slide. Stricken and yet curiously unmoved, restless and yet strangely at peace (because she is doing she knows what she always should have done), Lena holds position while the dead stalks through all the corridors of her being, first prodding, then poking, inspecting and massaging areas of consciousness, then, this preliminary done, having satisfied itself with the fact that she is a proper arena, the dead begins to speak with her. She lets this happen because, from having no time at all, she has turned to all the time necessary, and however long it takes to talk with the dead, she will control the chronology. When it is time to take *Skipstone* out, she will do so. She feels no urgency whatsoever. Doubt has been resolved. There is a kind of pitiless, bloodless joy to blending finally with what she has always known must happen.

"Just listen here," the dead says.

"I'm listening."

"Let me explain everything to you."

"No one can explain everything."

"With the dead all is known."

"All right," she says then, "all right."

"You believe that I can tell you everything or you would not have summoned me."

"That is not true," she says, "that is true."

Perhaps one should characterize this dead before moving further, individuate him in some way. It is not necessary to do this in order to make the full force of the dialogue apparent, but the dead, no less than the living, are entitled to characterization, and it is not intended here to slight him.

He was born—this is a male—in 3361, died in 3401, five hundred and one years ago. Cancer of the bone killed him at the age of forty. For some twenty-five generations, now, this dead has been embalmed, and yet despite all that has happened since, he submitted himself to the stasis of the machinery; despite all that has happened in the time intervening, not very much has happened at all. This is not a fluid society. Very few social and cultural changes can be said to have occurred in a millennium.

So certainly, brought to consciousness with the rest of the cargo when *Skipstone* hit the field, he has had ample time to pick up on any details which he might have missed through the period of stasis, and he has also been able to make certain linguistic adjustments, semantic reassessments which enable him to communicate with Lena spontaneously and in the vernacular of her day. His name, of course, does not matter; his name is *dead*, his characterization is formed by his condition. All, the memorial services remind us, all are the same in death: the wise man, the fool, the rich man in the palace and the poor man in his hovel, all of them, fallen asleep like a child over his toys, have let go of their earthly possessions and are now the same. But for all of that, for all the leveling of death, it is a hard and unique characterization which would make this dead significantly different from any of the others. The personality will always reach for itself. Under any conditions short of crisis, we will strive for difference; the brutalizing effects of tyranny are that these effects permit the differences to be shut off . . . a secret known to tyrants.

"Listen here to me," he says again, "and I'll put the full and final truth of this to you."

"That's why you're here." She speaks in a rather dull and abstracted fashion, her glance frozen inward to confront the dead as if he were some aspect of herself. Is he? This is a theme which the novel cannot touch. "If I didn't understand what was happening here, you never would have been summoned."

"Nonsense," the other says briskly. "That's easy sophistry, and while it may work with those other fools, you're not going to manage it with me. I'm not like them at all. Remember, I've already passed over the edge. You're only going to get the truth from me. There's nothing else."

"What's the truth?"

"The truth is that you cannot possibly leave here."

"I'm going to try," she says.

"I didn't say that you couldn't *try*. You may well succeed in breaking from the field, your thinking is correct on that issue, there may be a means of exit. But what I'm saying is that you can't do it because it's only going to make things much worse."

"Impossible. Nothing could be worse."

"Not impossible but quite true. Better the death we know than the death that you want to give us. The one is eternal and we can dwell within it. The other is final and will cancel all possibility of time."

"The decision is made," Lena says. Her fingers clamp against one another; she adopts an earnestly penitential position. "It has been made and there will be no turning back from this."

"We are dead now. At least let this death continue. At least in the field of this galaxy where there is no time at all we have a kind of life or at least we have that nullity of which we have always dreamed. I wish I could tell you some of the things that we have learned together during these seventy thousand years of perceived time, but they would make no sense to you."

"How do you know?"

"There is no order."

"Everything is ordered," Lena says; "everything, ultimately, does make sense."

Her tone is so flat, so deprived of affect, that she might be dead herself. One must understand the degree to which she has reached an absolute communion with her cargo. She sees no disparity between her position and theirs. In a way she wishes that she did, because if she could see herself as different from the dead, she would not be faced with the need she feels to persuade the spokesman that she is right. But she is one of them, and what she does to them, then, she does to herself.

She knows that to share with the dead, to understand them, is to pass the last of all barriers. To understand that in the jaws of the universe biting down hard, biting down harder, more toward blankness, that aberration known as humanity is so slight as to make even discrimination between its living and dead components no more significant than the differentiation one might make between the halves of an amoeba in mitosis. Living and dead, they have been joined in this everlasting and terrible vault, and she wishes somehow that she could make the dead understand this, too.

But he would not. Not ever. The pain of the dead is even greater, she supposes, than the pain of the living, and their bitterness, too, must increase. So all that she can do now is to listen submissively although her heart itself would scream, and if she could embrace this man, this dead, this specter, this craziness, she would, only to hold him against the anguish. But here is an irrationality, she knows, of such dimension that even in these altered circumstances she would not try to explain it. Certain things can never be understood, can never be confronted, but must be put from all of us. In that is the beginning of implication.

She faces the dead, voyaging within her to find the part where it has spoken, still without face and says, "I know what you are going to say."

"Do you? Do you really? Then do you know that we have found resignation, and can you even understand what resignation would be to us?"

"Yes, I know that."

"Do you know what is meant by the peace that passeth all understanding? Do you grasp what I am trying to say to you for all of us?"

"Yes," she says, "I know of that. I know of the peace that passes understanding."

"Passed. It's Biblical."

"All right. Biblical. I seek it in my way, and that is why we must leave, for there is no peace here."

"It is perfect. There is perfect and complete peace."

"That is an illusion. You have suffered greatly, and you prefer what we have found to the possibility of more suffering. But there is no accommodation. There is no way in which this can be adjusted to. Time is infinite but our own capacities are not. We will fall and fall. Forever."

"Toward oblivion."

"No. Toward madness."

"This is already madness."

"No, oblivion," she says; "that is what you do not see. We would have lost control, we would be utterly mad, and yet for the rest of all time we would know this, and that is what I cannot bear and why we must leave. Whatever the risk."

"You cannot measure the risk."

"This is merely a transitional stage. It is not the last which has been planned for us. If we do not get out, things will become even more terrible."

"No, they would not. We have gone through the other end; we are already dead and know the difference."

"You do not know madness or what they have in store for us. You understand none of that. None of it."

"You have no right to say that. That is merely arrogance. Once dead we have passed through to the realization of all."

"No," she says. She would stake everything on this denial. "No, that is not so."

"Are *you* dead?"

"We are the same here."

"Yes, but have you died?"

"I don't know. Who can tell? I know what we have passed through together, and I have seen much more than death."

"No," the dead says, "you are terribly wrong there. You have misunderstood utterly. There are absolutes," he says; "damn it, damn you, there are absolutes after all," and then he seems able, at least momentarily, to say no more.

XLI

The speed of light is one hundred and eighty-six thousand miles a second, which would seem to be fast enough, and yet in astronomical terms, in terms of space exploration, it would be the Seventh Avenue local with brake trouble.

It takes, for instance, more than four years for light to travel from the nearest star, Proxima Centauri, to the Earth, about nine or ten times that for light to travel from Sirius, which we take to be virtually the nearest star with the possibility of a planetary system and conditions that might support our own kind of life. Just in the Milky Way, that corner of the galaxy occupied by Sol, thousands of years elapse in the passage of light from one side to the next. There are galaxies whose light we now see is the expression of energy emitted hundreds of thousands of years ago.

And far beyond the realm of sight or even the most powerful telescopes lie the pulsars, believed to be the waves of energy emitted by galaxies at such inconceivable distance that their light has not reached us, may not reach us for millennia, may never reach us at all, because by the time their light has traveled here, Sol itself may have died, and the Earth may be a burned pellet circling the ruined star. Or may have been absorbed in the final explosion.

Consider these two factors: the dimension of the universe and the impossibility of tracking it through any speeds up to the speed of light. The Bureau had to consider them in the early years of the fourth millennium, just as science fiction writers of our own day had had to deal with them. It might have served the purposes of the Bureau if it had had access to these texts . . . but of course none of them existed.

(No records remained of that period toward the end of the second millennium. There was not a single scrap of evidence showing how the folk of that time had dealt with their problem, not even a sacred scroll embodying the words of the followers enshrined in some buried museum of artifacts. All of it had been destroyed much earlier, as if someone in the eras succeeding that millennium had made a unilateral decision that there should be no trace whatsoever of the past. Civilization appears to have been virtually reconstructed beginning around the year 2200; there is little bridge between that second era and all that preceded.

(Nor had there been such a museum, a collection of artifacts, would they have been closely observed. This is a notably phlegmatic and unsentimental age, without any sense of history or interest in pursuing a past deemed irrelevant. Human endeavor is cyclical, and there was a period in the 2500s when archaeology flourished: there was a stochastic frenzy and a desperate interest in finding how civilization had once destroyed itself through technology so that it would not happen again, and there had been a tyranny of researchers which had led to colorful and vicious episodes of political brutality, proving that historians and archaeologists were no less intrinsically violent than those who cared not of the past. But the 2500s are quaint now, have long passed into anonymity, and little traces of that civilization likewise remain. In the year 3902 there are virtually no archaeologists.)

That problem the Bureau faced was the development of a practical, faster-than-light drive.

The galaxy, let alone the universe, could not be colonized without it. It is impossible to conceive of any flight that could last hundreds or thousands of years without the descendants of the original crew having lost any sense of mission, any desire for completion, any understanding of origin, and, furthermore, there is no level of alienation as complete as to make competent people consent to spending the remainder of their lives in a ship moving at impossible but still finite speeds toward an unknown destination. People could not even be bred for this, although there were some rather horrid experiments conducted at mental institutions hundreds of years ago.

Accordingly, the Bureau researchers had to understand, man's tenuous efforts to populate or at least chart the universe which had moved at geometric rate through the conquest of the Centaurus and even toward the initial hold on Sirius—thirty-six years to the hardy explorers of that time was just barely feasible, what with the enormous bonuses the Bureau paid as well as the parole from death sentences—would come to a complete stop. Science fiction writers of this time, then, were not the only group that could not deal with that possibility. The Bureau writhed under it as well. How was it going to evolve a drive that would bring it the stars? How would it get around the chronological gap? What was the point in having a Bureau at all? What was the point in evolving interplanetary travel and sophisticated devices of colonization and exploration if they were cut off at a given point? The Bureau might have to dissolve. This was impossible, since in certain crucial senses, ways which the population did not entirely understand, the Bureau ran the world.

The work of Einstein had been buried with that of all his contemporaries, but his work was painfully reconstructed by physicists of the 3500s who worked independently, as if Einstein had never existed. Like him, they postulated at first that faster-than-light travel was impossible under all terms of conceptually grasped Euclidean physics. As speed approached that of light, these neo-Einsteinian theories of relativity held; mass and time would dwindle inversely so that a ship traveling right up to the speed of light (and never exactly at it, since it could only be approached, not met) would remain in static time at microscopic size. When it decelerated and reached its destination, the occupants would find that hundreds, perhaps thousands of years had passed while they had undergone only the relative time span of the trip. Thirty-six years to Sirius, then, only to find oneself utterly separate from the culture he had left!

Of course this would not matter on Sirius, but it would matter very much indeed in terms of obtaining contact with the culture from which you had left. Would it have kept proper records of your flight or would it have disappeared under another millennial frenzy?

During the course of the Bureau's cautious experimentation through the mid- to late thirties, it was found that this part, at least, of the relativity equation did not apply. Crews did not become microscopic nor did time pass at a shuddering and insurmountable rate outside of the space capsule. What the neo-Einsteinians had postulated just did not check out to the relief, of course, of the Bureau.

But the other significant section of the relativity theory did appear to hold. Although a faster-than-light drive might have been theoretically possible under non-Euclidean physics, no one could make it practical. The speed of light could not be exceeded. And a ship walled in by that upper limit might as well not be traveling—in terms of cosmic exploration—at all.

It was then that the Bureau embarked upon its long, secret and dangerous experiments in search of a hyperdrive, one that would indeed exceed the speed of light. At the time of this novel, the bureaucracy, as the reader can well sense, had long since fallen into decadence, self-contempt, rigidified forms and custom, but it would do discredit to the brilliant and courageous researchers and voyagers of this early time who were responsible for the great days of an institution that for the last five hundred years had merely been moving on the inertial impact of those energies. The experiments went forward; they caused great loss of life and circumstance, but they can be said to have given man the universe. They opened up the possibility of the faster-than-light drive.

That drive was predicated upon tachyonic force: the conversion, that is, of the constituent ions of the ship to particles which assumed the qualities of faster-than-light atoms. These atoms are different in all of their properties from those of the "normal" universe, although they can be reconstituted. The atoms, in short, can change their condition.

That was the most brilliant insight of the Bureau researchers and voyagers in those early days . . . that they were able to change the literal constituent qualities of atoms so that a ship could slip in and out of the field of faster-than-light drive in some exact reclamation of its original form. There was less trouble in sending a ship into hyperspace than in getting it out in its original condition. That could only be accomplished by a trial-and-error process which was, to be sure, intermittently disastrous.

There were failures: experiments which resulted in hideous effects upon those returned in different form or no form at all, grotesques shambling from the converters, creatures which were of no universe we can name seen in the force fields shimmering before return, destroyed by the technicians before they could come out . . . and of these failures as much should be written as of the successes, for only through failure can humanity transcend itself. Success teaches nothing; failure presents limits, gives us the tragic sense without which understanding is impossible. Successes are composed of a thousand failures like the way the photos in newspapers reduce on inspection to myriad scattered dots, each expressionless, all comprising vision. And of the Bureau in those middle years of the fourth millennium, a great and grave instrument, something must be written and someday will because this is a history accessible to many.

The author may charge himself to the task. What is a body of work in our field without somewhere tucked in a future history? The idea of a future history may seem frivolous: after all, it might well be presumptuous to sketch a future when too few of us have any grasp whatsoever of the past let alone the present, and if we cannot comprehend our future without a sense of history, then science fiction must be the least relevant of all branches of literature. And then again, assuming that we will never possess our history (the people of 3902 have utterly lost theirs), assuming that our history is being eradicated through event and in our culture has become almost instantaneous, certainly always contemptible . . . then if that is the case, perhaps the future can replace the past. By knowing where we thought we might go, we can reconstruct what we might have been. One will work as well as the other. Chronology is only a function of personality-in-culture. One may, scratching out didacticism where it can be found, take on a new kind of cunning.

So there might at some time be other works which will paint in some of the gaps only suggested here. The struggles of the Bureau to perfect the hyperdrive in the face of the pain, the losses, the ships that never returned and those which did in altered form and those few, gallant stragglers which by docking in the Antares system or traversing corners of the Milky Way proved that it was possible that the tachyons could hold matter as well as the tardyons and that the only barriers which held man to his limitations were self-erected.

There are stories here of schemes and wonder: the courage of the Bureau and many of those who, seeing what the Bureau would become when the struggles were over, did all they could to subvert it, but, losing, did away with themselves. There are the stories of the lost ships and the monsters within, some who sacrificed themselves willingly when they could have returned and exposed themselves to the world, brought about the end of the program in revulsion. Most of those stories would do more credit to the Bureau than what does exist here. But it would not be entirely fair to the Bureau to judge it by what it has become; not fair either to judge history either by the point that it has reached in 3902. There is much to be said, then, which can only be inferred here; there will be time, later on, to go back and to pick out, chiaroscuro fashion, notes toward a larger and more definitive series of novels which will explore the history of the Bureau from the days of origin until its bleak and somehow pathetic end in the year 4911 when its total membership had been reduced to four.

But not now, of course, not now: there is the instant situation with which to deal and that is certainly more than enough. Lena through *Skipstone* has not been testing the tachyonic drive—that has already been known and stabilized for several hundred years—but modification on the tachyons which would enable them to carry a much larger payload at the same speed, a payload, to be sure, mostly concerned with loading more of the dead aboard, getting greater cargo, greater remuneration. The more dead the more income the larger the payload and the more dead . . . or at least this is the circularity in which the Bureau—which I hope has been made clear by this time is a rather tragic institution—has gotten itself trapped.

At the beginning there were plans to carry larger crews on the FTL, having larger and more diversified colonization teams than had been true in the past, but early on, when the principle of financing pay-as-you-go through the dead had been evolved, it seemed to the Bureau that it would be better to outfit the ships with dead rather than living. This may show a certain dimness of thought, shortsightedness on its part, but then again the Bureau is decadent and running a decadent age. In 3619 it would have been inconceivable for someone as casually qualified as Lena Thomas to have been in solitary command of a piece of equipment as complex as *Skipstone.* There would have been a crew of at least a half-dozen, and she would have been no more than fifth in seniority. But more living would have been here, fewer dead, and it is the dead who have made the program possible. One must leave metaphysical considerations out of this. Only spiritual reasoning, if that is the word, could apply, for in the Bureau's estimation the dead have become the living and the living merely dead space, using up resources that could be better assigned to several of the more economically stacked dead.

At ten point eight million miles per second, *Skipstone* has moved in free fall, searching the arms of the spiral galaxy until caught by the neutron star and sent with its dead into the pit that will end time. And in a way this is all the Bureau's fault, for the experiments themselves and for failing to take proper precautions, for not having anticipated the possibility of the black galaxy. But in another way it is not the fault of the Bureau at all.

It has nothing to do with the Bureau, has nothing to do with anything except preordination and the shaping hand of the author, because it was always destined—one can find this out for sure by correctly interpreting the prophecies contained in the Book of Daniel—for time to end in this seventh month of the year 3902, three thousand nine hundred and six years since the birth of the Saviour and a few more dozens of centuries past that from the second destruction of the temple which rendered the Jews forever a scattered people, wanderers and exiles like the FTL ship, probing the crevices of space for something which they could occupy. But there is little mysticism about the Judaic condition, something which cannot be said about what has happened to *Skipstone*.

XLII

"It would be apostasy to leave here," the dead says. All the time that the author has been laboring through his expository creaks and joints, the dead and Lena have still been trying to work things out, locked in their confrontation in *Skipstone* which will go utterly to resolution without extrinsic pressure because there is no time here. "You must stay. You owe that obligation not only to us, but also to yourself. In what form do you think you will be when you emerge? Have you opened that issue to your heart? Do you understand what you might become?"

"Yes," Lena says, "I have thought of that, I have thought of everything without you. And it does not matter. It does not matter what form I will take. Nothing matters."

"Everything matters. Everything affects everything else in an endless chain of consequence. I have made you; you are the product of all the dead, just as you in turn will be the product of those who will make us. Life does not exist in cubicles but only in terms of what it inhabits."

"I know that."

"There is an endless chain of consequence of which everyone is a link. You must accept that."

"I do," Lena says. She has entered a mystical, almost penitential frame of mind. Nothing can touch her. She feels easy; her joints seem to glide, she has an impression of herself as a physical being which she has not had in a long time. "I do understand. I am not stupid. Nor am I dead."

"Of course you aren't," the dead says rather vaguely. He seems to be discombobulated, but this may only be the shift of vapors in the hold, impossible to say. Confidence drains from him; he seems to take on a rather imploring tone as if he had realized that the right of decision had passed to Lena, which, of course, it has. "That has nothing to do with it. Who said that you were dead?"

Twitches of the pain which sent him into the vault, closed down the windows of his mortality, assault him then; he feels an old weakness which is composed not only of metaphysical spite but seems to occupy a physical plane. "Please," he says, "I don't know what you're talking about now. I really don't know what you want. How can you try to leave? Are you possessed? If you do, then it will surely destroy us all."

"So be it. We need destruction."

"It may even destroy time. Have you thought of that? You may shake the balance of the universe. You may end all time as we comprehend it. Have you thought of doing this? Would you end everything?"

"Let the universe take care of itself."

"What a selfish answer."

"What a *human* answer. Why do I have to think of the fate of the universe? That's only an excuse for the truth. The truth is what becomes of me."

"Is your vanity so great?"

"Great enough," she says, "great enough." Then she attempts to put everything which she has so perilously learned in terms so simple that even this obdurate dead can understand. "We are obligated to try. We must do the best we can for ourselves. If we do that, the universe will follow. We cannot be concerned with the universe; our concern is our own fate."

"Nonsense."

"We fell in, we must get out."

"Not we. Just you."

"All of us carry within ourselves the totality of humanity. We must reconstruct our history at every moment. Man must struggle, attempt to control the conditions that oppress him."

"Even if they cannot be controlled?"

"Only the dead believe that," she says, "but the living are not the dead and that is the difference, the belief that we can control. Isn't that the only difference between us? And even if it's only a passage from struggle to oblivion, that still is a kind of destiny. Isn't it?"

"You are a fool. You are saying that you know you will become the dead. We wait for you. All of your struggles are toward that end. But if you know the answer, if you know your fate, then what is the point of the struggle?"

"No point," she says. "That must be left in judgment out of the equation. Since we cannot understand death, it is of no matter what revelation it must hold. We must struggle as if death were merely a transitional stage."

"Bullshit," the dead man says. "You are a fool. Now you will destroy everything."

"But it's life."

"This is life?"

"It isn't death," she says, "and if we can't hold onto that difference then what, tell me, what is the meaning of any of this?"

And the music of the fall overwhelms her as the dead does not answer. *The dead does not answer.* There is nothing, at last, to say.

XLIII

"I'm afraid," she said to John at some point in her training, impossible to localize the time, but then she had always been afraid. She can admit that now; she had entered the Bureau in fear, and fear magnified had been all of growth that she knew. "I don't want to go. I don't like what they're doing to us here. It isn't right."

"It's merely your fear of the unknown," he said to her. Perhaps they were twined together in bed somewhere, perhaps they were having this discussion under the cool high glare of circuitry in some public place. It does not matter. He leaned forward, put his cheek against her, and she felt the arching slab of his face as he spoke. "It's natural, it's normal to feel this way. Put it under the name of xenophobia. The atavism of the savage, the fear of that which he feels he cannot control. You can conquer it; you will be able to deal with it if you only will. All of that is to be expected and they have taken it into account."

"It isn't right," she said, "it isn't right. Can't I make you see that it isn't right?"

"Right doesn't matter."

"They don't know what's going on there, and they're merely using us for experimentation." She shook against him; he touched her but was cold, cold now, his body shadows and clutching. She could not see his eyes. "But they won't let me stop now, will they?" she said. "That's for sure."

"No," he said, "no, there's no turning back, and you wouldn't want to anyway; this is where you should be, this is what you should be doing," and thought that he had lied, this was not normal; she was, in fact, at a dangerous point where she might go now in either direction. She might retreat into panic and refuse to take the *Skipstone* out and in that case what would the Bureau do? She may have no legal right of refusal, but it could hardly send a reluctant pilot. There have, in the past, been commanders who had refused, ultimately, to partake of the voyages, but none of them had taken hold of anything as significant as this, had had this large a cargo or that much of an investment in the voyage. "Don't worry about it," John said, feeling futile, and held her more tightly, reaching for some affectional basis (he hated himself for thinking in this way, but that was what the Bureau had delegated him to do), the aftermath of sex and its ruined fires like a damp wall crumbling between them but trying to force her by pressure into an accommodation which reason itself might not accomplish.

"Everything will be all right," he said. "The training goes satisfactorily, you are doing well, you should be without fear. All will work out for the best, and you will be glad, at the end, that you have done this."

"The dead," she said. "The dead." She held herself against him, her hands up and down the running surfaces of his body, and John, trembling underneath, felt the touch of those hands open him to a kind of darkness which he could not comprehend but which would penetrate him, he knew, to levels that he had never before touched, a pain which went to the very core of his relationship with the Bureau and which took him into areas he was simply not equipped to handle. (For all of his superficial intelligence and charm, he was really quite limited, and he has just enough intelligence to know this.) He pushed her away from him and said then, "I don't know what you're talking about," even though he did. "Please, Lena; you must stop this now. It does nothing for us." Something like fear coiled within him. He had never before thought of the emotional significance of carrying the dead, vaulting a cargo of corpses at unspeakable speed. *What would it do to one, what did it really mean?* He did not want to think any more of this.

"The dead," she said again, her eyes closed against the light of her vision, "that's the purpose of this mission; there is no other. To convey the dead, to carry them. Everything else, the tachyonic drive, the search for new galaxies, the colonization rationale are merely excuses. Why won't they tell us the truth? Everything is for the dead and what they have given us."

"No," John said, "not for the dead but the living," but he did not believe this, when all was finally at conclusion, he knew then as he always would that he was not a fool and what he said was so obviously untrue, so pointless and equivocating as against the simple power of her statement, that he could hardly take himself seriously much less the attempts that he made then to soothe and quiet her, holding her against him, talking to her deeply, intensely, trying to communicate through touch and tone what words would not bring.

"For the living," he said, "only for the living," and she said, "No, for the dead; that was the way that they always wanted it, to find a way to deal with the dead, and if they ever solved that problem then they would be committed to death," and at the end of this it would be only weariness which brought them together, not passion, their opposition welded, dead and living, living and dead, meshed over all the spaces of the pallet on which once again they entered one another because in this year 3902, just as today except more so, because of the decadence and rigid formulations of those times, sex was sought as a release from the tensions and pressures of the common existence, although it only led more often than not to frustration, doubt, misery and loss, this being one of the numerous ironies played upon the race by the conditions of its mortality.

Living and dead, dead and living, the scent of them flowing on the hard, brown, surrounding husk of their union.

XLIV

Eager to make his argument, eager for once to make the issues clear and without the masking of characterization, the author has been in such haste to hurl didacticism at the reader that intention may be too forthright. Expository material, individuating touches have been scrapped in these concluding sections; the dialogue has become florid. It need not, for example, have been so compressed; it might have been useful to have moved away from such philosophic or metaphysical intensity, to have described yet again the interior of the cabin, the appearance of the prostheses, the sensations of falling, the sound of the engines, the whispers of the dead. Also, one could have woven in detail the past life of the dead with whom she has had her final argument, certain details of his biography, rowdy and solemn by turns, to give him a warm, human aspect, the actual physical projection of him which she sees mentally, the way in which she reacts to this vision as contrasted to and compared with the way that she reached her lover/superior John. Once again the old equation between sex and death, so popular in modern literature, could have been a serviceable metaphor for the argument that passes between them.

Impatient for once, however, I have scrapped these details for the more abstract. Issues are more important than people in science fiction, and even that kind of science fiction which devotes relative attention to characterization or pain must, when confronted with the ultimate necessity to *keep things scientific*, move away from the matter of humanity. If you want to write about people, you had better stay away from this format; this is a truth taken to heart by everyone who has ever worked successfully, within the form, and the author is no exception; he is involved with the effects here. The neutron star comes as close to a protagonist as this novel will ever have.

This is not to say that the intention all along was a disguised lecture in astrophysics and time. I am certainly no less interested in metaphor, description, idiosyncrasy, structure than a writer of any routine literary bent . . . but the arguments of *Galaxies* can best be accomplished through letting the rags of didacticism flutter, however drably, in the breeze of dialogue. If this will alienate some readers, well then, again, it will be of attraction to others. Science fiction readers have historically shown themselves more willing to settle for straight factual presentation and argument than the readers of any other class of popular literature.

Indeed, many of us modern-type science fiction writers have been criticized for ignoring the intellectual interests of our readers, failing to provide them with a nourishing diet of ideas to complement the technical displays and characteriological evasions with which so much of the literature of the field has been recently concerned. That being so—of course it is so—I can hardly be criticized for having been so straightforward in these chapters. Indeed, I have taken the instructions of those critics to heart and, for once, am doing it their way. The argument is certainly the core of this novel, for if it is not, then there cannot, by any means, be an emotional effect.

No, the author busily wants this to be a freak show, one of his characteristic productions of sleazy wonders shown giggling and peeping back at the onlookers through the tent of purpose; he does not want this to be yet another display of idiosyncrasy but instead a solid and thoughtful attempt to limn out a future history arching toward the end of time, setting up the base pivot which has caused all of this to happen. The end of the universe cannot, should not, be done within the context of the freak show. A certain decorum is called for. Nothing should be done below the literary waist. One must not take liberties. One should not seek to titillate but to appeal to the intellectual faculties of the reader, for the reader must have respect for the writer if anything is to come through. We must not violate one another.

And if nothing else, the writer is confident that, having come to this point, the reader with him, he has at least gained the respect of the reader. He knows that the author's intentions are pure, that he will not, at the least, be violated. What after all is the writer but the reader's creation, helping him to construct collaboratively that ultimately satisfying novel which he seeks to leave the place where he has been? It is a long flight; the reader needs all the help available to get through this one. He can almost but not quite do it by himself.

And the author has been a deferential guide: slow, sincere, a little pedantic and inclined toward self-mockery, but he has revealed himself while asking no revelations in turn (and thereby foregoing catharsis) but merely the grim knowledge that, if it were not for this, the novel could not work at all. He is sure that his honesty will be rewarded. The reader will make allowances for any obscurities; he will go along at this stage. Because if those allowances are not made, you see, all of this has been pointless . . . much as if Lena is wrong in her determination and decision, then the novel itself must be without point.

"You see," she says almost conversationally, her emotion drained by the anguish of what she has said, what she has had to fight through to have reached that knowledge, "you see, I don't care about the dead. My concern is for the living among us."

"What living? Just yourself?"

"For all of us."

"If you care only for the living," the dead man says, winking one, large, bleak eye in the center of the ruined forehead, this new form one with which she is comfortable, meeting and mocking her perception of him as utterly vile, "if you care for the living, then you must show some concern for the universe itself which contains all of the living."

"The universe is of the dead."

"Now that would be an alternative universe, one which you could not conceive, could not know of. The universe in which you live holds only life. And do you know what can happen if you try to come through it?"

"No. Of course not. Nor do you."

"But I am not seeking to do it. You have to have concern for what may happen."

"Ah, well," she says, "we will just find out. We will find out what happens because we will go through it."

"I will tell you," the dead says, "I will tell you what could happen. No one can be absolutely sure of this, but this is as close as one can come to true suggestion. By going through the center of the black hole, which is what will happen when you switch to tachyons without transition, you will rupture the seamless fabric of space and time themselves. Normal considerations which you hold do not apply. The effect of the tachyonic switch will be absolutely calamitous; you will fall through, and you will destroy space and time itself, the totality ripped."

"If I don't know that how can you?"

"Because there are layers of knowledge open to the dead which cannot be shared by the living. Everything will be destroyed."

"Why don't I hear from any other of the dead? Why just from you?"

"I am their spokesman."

"Who decided?"

"Through my voice you hear many voices. Through my voice you hear all voices. The explosion working against the implosion of the star may extend the funnel of gravitational forces to infinite proportion."

The dead pauses, blinks his eye, seems to investigate the images evoked by what he has just said. "All of the universe will fall through that hole," he says, "and all of time as well. Time will reconstruct itself but only in the abyss. You will never know what you have done, because you will never move past that point. Do you know what that means, then? You will relive this over and again. So you will never leave. Never. You will be in anguish forever, reenacting this constancy over and again."

Lena shakes her head. If she is jolted, she will not show it at any level which the dead can apprehend (although, she thinks, this is foolish because the dead can apprehend everything). "All right," she says, "that's terrible. But it still makes no difference." She will yield nothing to this creature. Nothing whatsoever. She will give no part of herself or feeling. The dead must be another of her tempters; the dead has become a fourth comforter in yet more cunning and outrageous guise. It is a plot. It is all a plot worked out by the Bureau to make her progressively confused and malleable. It never had her interests at heart. Now it does not want her to return and expose it. She must believe this. She must hold onto this, because if she does not, she has gone through all of this exactly nowhere and seventy thousand years have had no significance.

"You are lying," she says.

"I cannot lie by definition."

"And even if it's the truth, so what? So who cares? You do not even exist; there is no reality to you. I hear your voice, but it is merely hallucinative. It is another effect of the neutron star; it has made me irrational."

"You are irrational."

"I am responsible only to myself. The universe is merely an excuse, an extension of my own personality and the *Skipstone*'s struggle. It is not an issue. It never was. It's only an excuse for doing things that are terrible."

"*That* makes no sense."

"It does!" she says desperately. "It does! It isn't a rationalization, it isn't an excuse. I know that this is the truth, that you're just trying to confuse me with talk of the universe, space and time because of my own fear of leaving, of taking the risk. I've no need to listen to you. You aren't telling me the truth. You can't be!"

"But I am," he says. He has seen her hesitation, scented her pain and feels as if old mysteries were moving the ruined blood against his victory. He knows that if he can pursue the advantage opened here they will never leave this galaxy, because in the end he has proven the stronger. The dead are stronger than the living always, he thinks, because they are destination. "You are rationalizing," he says; "you will not confront the truth. You know it now as well as I do. You cannot avoid it."

"No."

"Yes. Yes! You can't be an utter solipsist, Lena, not here, not even under seventy thousand years of the lash. You aren't God, there is no God, not here."

"Yes, there is. There must be a God."

"If there was, He would not be here. This is dead space, this is null time. This is that from which the universe was created. This is before the beginning."

"That's evil to say. If there is a God, He would be everywhere, certainly here."

"Would He? Do you really believe that? This is the truth. You must measure this universe by yourself; that is the only faith that you can ever find, the only constancy that you will ever know. You can look for no one, nothing else."

The dead has said this triumphantly, his inner voice arching through a shout. He knows that he has won. She looks at him and he looks at Lena and in that confrontation, in the shade of his one, clouded eye as his glance passes through the dull illumination of the neutron star, she sees that they are close to a communion so terrible that it will become a weld, will be a true connection. If she listens to this dead for even another instant, she will collapse within those features as *Skipstone* has collapsed into the black hole, and she cannot bear this. It cannot be.

No, it cannot be; she must preserve herself at all costs. She must hold onto her individuation, the feeling that she is right, that she has at all costs won through to an epiphany worth the having and that the separation between the living and the dead is real, that it will hold and that there will be dignity in that situation. Life, she thinks, life is not death, because if that is so, there is no point in having struggled. If she believes that, she denies herself and all the becoming necessary for her to be here.

XLV

So she does not consider further. She will not think because to give thought is submission. Quickly she moves toward the controls, the levers of power which when hit will convert the ship instantly past the speed of light, and then in the explosions of many suns that might only be the illumination of the network of pain within her, she hides her head in her arms. She screams.

Screams not for herself but for the dead, not for the dead but for all the cargo, the lusterless, gelatinous forms lying in the hold, slipping like fish through the ocean of space: now she sees them, holds onto them in a sense of fusion unlike anything she has known before. They are not *the* but *her* dead, all of them, gliding in and out in a sleek possession harder and brighter than anything, almost as if all of them have been massed to plead with her.

"Oh, no," she says, for the pain is quite inexpressible, and she has been reduced to simple moans and murmurs. "Oh, no, it can't be. Something like this cannot be."

"Yes," the dead says, stronger now even though knowledge of his defeat has suddenly seeped through him in the backwash of victory; he does not quite understand how this has happened to him, and yet loss seems to renew him as victory never would; he has the strength drawn from doom. "Yes, this is what has happened. This is the way that it will be."

"It's too terrible."

"All of us with you, Lena. All of us. No separation, just the complete binding."

"I never wanted it this way. I didn't want—"

"It could have been no other."

"Please—"

"Yes," she says, "yes."

They speak to one another now in the short, abbreviated barks of lovers, little stumps of words and thought. They might indeed be lovers intertwined on a bed rather than on the canopy of space. *Please. No. Yes. Will. Won't. Ahoy. Help. Now. Later.* The murmurs of exchange pass between them like the darker and older coins of love. She finds herself too weary to continue and yet she must. She finds that she cannot go on and yet she continues. If she does not, then it has all been futile. She wants not only his acceptance—which acceptance he could never have denied—but his understanding. Can she make this clear to him? Can she communicate? "I want to live," she says, "that's all, live."

"All did. All do."

"I have a right to live."

"Not at the cost of time."

"At any cost. At any cost at all."

"Life should not only be an expression of selfishness."

"It must be. You're wrong. In order to persist, it has to be. Otherwise I would be dead. No one would have ever lived. Life itself would not exist."

"It is your decision, Lena." Centuries of anguish have flowed through him like water, just since she pushed the levers; now he has nothing left. He cannot continue the disputation. Whatever it is, it is over. "It was always your decision, if you wanted to do it. No one can change you. You can never be changed."

"No matter the cost."

"You have made it that way."

"Yes," she says, "yes. I have made it that way. I want it, I want eviction from this galaxy. I want the sun again, I want light I want this, I want that, I want, I want—"

She stops. She throws back her head. And then she screams.

And the dead screams, too; it is not a cry of accomplishment or joy, but not of terror either; this must be understood; what comes out of this, what comes from the two of them, is the true natal cry suspended, as it were, in these moments of limbo. Life and expiration become fused here, their shrieks intertwine much as all the themes of the novel can be said at this point to blend, and if the work has been done well, the reader at this point should feel a real jolt of terror, terror of recognition, of course. Then in the womb of *Skipstone* they continue to scream in a rhythmic fashion, the shrieks entwined as the ship pours through the redeemed and climactic light.

XLVI

We are upon the conclusion and that conclusion, obviously, is open-ended.

Cunningly it has been built into the construct from the very outset. It is a characteristic of a certain kind of well-structured fiction that it will lead toward a resolution which in retrospect may appear inevitable but which in fact is only one of a series of choices which could have been made and which, in the fact of its selection, has become the trans-mutative force of the work, has cast back little slices of light from which the novel, read once again, may acquire additional depth. The proper ending for the writer, then, is not so much constructed as *discovered*. It is a matter of working through the material consciously or subconsciously so that the ending is seen retrospectively as having been in place all along, not to be recognized until the point of its organic extension from the material.

This is not quite such a construction, alas; the ending could go any way at all, much as could *Skipstone*. It would be hard to write a tight resolution, an elegantly structured novel given the material here. With nothing less than all possibility as its field, how could *Galaxies* cleanly seize one from a set of alternatives as to make it appear that there were none other?

No, anything at all can happen here. The novel, many-leveled and certainly provocative in premise if not characterization, would yield to a number of endings. Only a few of them can be suggested here. Let them represent a much larger number.

Perhaps, then, Lena emerges once again into her own time and space. She finds that all of the events in the black galaxy have merely been a concealing sheath over the greater reality.

"I see," she would say as she flicked into normal space a hundred light years from Sirius, the breath of her anticipation cooling in her chest, all voices silenced, "I see now, I see what they wanted to do. It is not fair," she would say, her eyes filling with stunned wonder at the audacity of the Bureau, at its cruelty. It was all a test. "It cannot be this way; they cannot do this to us; we have more importance than they give us credit for having," and so on and so forth, the force of her discovery taking her almost all the way to madness and then back again as the ship on automatic settles toward its predetermined docking where the experiments would swarm and pull from *Skipstone* every last scrap of data embedded on those tapes, the tapes a full recording of all the interesting events just as the Bureau had hoped in setting up its ultimate stress reaction as Lena herself, a muttering husk, is committed to the deepest, institutional abscess of the Bureau where for the next several years she might lie under the electrodes, being at last gutted. Not a happy conclusion, this, not happy at all, and yet one can see that she has gotten what she deserved all the time. The Bureau, having manipulated the conquest of space for more than a millennium, would hardly have allowed the ship to fall into a black galaxy: the only black galaxy that would exist would be one prepared by the simulators. So much for metaphysics. So much for the seriousness of the issues raised. It was all an experiment, and the decadent Bureau has decadently manipulated her, to say nothing of the reader, only to find out to what limits its technicians will sustain their humanity. Knowing those limits, they can then easily move past them.

That is one ending; another might see Lena emerging into an otherness. One moment she is being torn through the black galaxy, in the next she finds herself in a gray space where all of time, light, depth, possibility have been suspended. In emptiness the tachyons strain, trying to lift the ship beyond. In perfect nullity the thing that was Lena stands rooted to the plates of the ship, waiting for that moment of stasis to pass, but this will never happen.

No, it cannot: she has fallen through the pit of the universe in the one moment of leap and now toward a state of denial, of anti-existence. One can see denial in her finger, her eyebrows, the desperate attempt of what was once her mouth and is now a horror to form words of prayer . . . but in this void words cannot be formed nor thoughts. In perfect stasis she stays there forever. She has no sensation of time passing nor does she have the sensation of it being instantaneous. She is not dead nor is she alive. She does not succeed nor does she fail. Mindlessly, she and the ship are imploded within to hold the moment in which she pushed the cruel lever home.

Maybe a monument is erected to her in memory of this; maybe at another time she becomes an artifact to be glimpsed by fascinated tourists who pass in and out of hyperspace on their tours, circling the black galaxy at a time infinitely advanced when the gravitational effects can at last be exploited. All of the universe may someday be an amusement park; Lena would be an exhibit well worth the trouble. Galactic Wonderburgers would be nearby. This ending would be flooded with warm, individuating touches to augment its irony; it would deal with the imperishability of man, his ability to make junk out of any part of the cosmos. Nothing can defy his trivialization, but that trivialization becomes in itself a profundity; it is a comment which makes as much sense, if not more, than a deification. Why deify the unknown if it can be manipulated, controlled, packaged and sold? Idolatry need not blind the eye; it may seem to sharpen it, lift that which it reflects to celebration.

And there might be another ending, here a construction in which Lena does escape. She emerges into a vortex of fire and is grabbed by the thrashing heart of a star, winking instantaneously into death along with all of her dead; they muddle and mingle together in a star song of extinction. So much here, then, for celestial exploration, so much for the broken spirit of man. So there for all of you, so *there*. All of the pain, the struggle for acquisition, the explanation and metaphor for nothing. A burst of epiphany and then obliteration. All of them overwhelmed and yet unthinking.

But, of course, of course, there are many such alternatives, and all of these must be passed over in pursuit of the real and true, the absolute conclusion which has not yet been stated.

XLVII

For, after all, not any ending will do. Not everything would fall into place, would be emotionally satisfying. The discovered ending which would be the truth is hard bought, but it is there, and I think that I have found it. The going has not been easy through any of this, and the climax has oozed rather than leaped from that canister of the unconscious to which it has been confined . . . but still, there it is, there it is now, and looking at it with mingled revulsion and awe, the author can do nothing but state it.

And it must be understood before that resolution is given that, just as these are merely a set of notes for a novel, so, similarly, the ending as conceived is just that, nothing more: a series of notes toward the conclusion. For the ending cannot be sculptured any more satisfactorily than the novel to which it is prefatory matter can be. It is simply too audacious, this, too broad, entirely too removed from the experience of even the most broad-minded of us. It can only be hinted, and perhaps circumvention is the way to get at this rather than using confrontation. What is there to say? What can be easily stated? If Lena's dilemma is immeasurably vast, then the way in which the novel comes to terms may simply be slight. Any outcome would seem trivial.

But, the resolution is there. It is viable. It is, in fact, inevitable. Emerging textually from the material, it has been hard bought, and perhaps one can see that it was, after all, implied from the very beginning, from the onset of these notes. The author has struggled, he has worked hard, he has done what he could to piece out this resolution. Give him, then, give him that ending.

The characters, too, deserve it.

XLVIII

For in the infinity of all time and all space, anything is possible if only once. Anything may happen if only at a given time, and as *Skipstone* trembles with the power of its transition, as time shifts and they are vomited from that black hole, Lena and her dead fall into infinity. They become bound to it. They scurry like the hand of a drunken painter over the vast canvas of all possibility, cleaving through the burlap of the galaxies.

Now here they are in the Antares Cluster, flickering like a bulb, the ship power shuddering as they plunge toward the dead star, and now here they are again momentarily at the heart of Sirius, the core heat a series of blows to the drowned metal; now yet again they move through some slip in time to find themselves in ancient Rome, possibly in an arena watching gladiators, brutish men with stupid faces reflecting pain, struggle in an abattoir, then moving in the air like some machine of prophecy watching another man haul wood up a high mountain . . .

And they do not know what they have seen, of course, certain myths being nonrecurring, traditions being reconstituted every few centuries, but even as they attempt to take in the significance of that, the ship moves again, shedding various levels of reality just as it sheds space and time, and they plunge a billion years across the flat, dead span of the universe, cling briefly to a hundred thousand habitable planets, and on each of them, infinity encompassing all, there is a mountain with a man carrying wooden bulk, and on each of them they see this, although memory is abolished along with context, and for each of them witness is as the first time. There is no history nor is there accumulation.

It is impossible to say how long this goes on or whether time can be said to apply to it at all. All that can be known is that *Skipstone* moves, and its occupants and author alike tremble on the verge of an epiphany and that epiphany is this: they cannot partake of the infinite; the equipment which receives this is so limited as to cancel consequence and we are after all merely human. We must reconstruct from all the pathways of the possible, then, that frail gestalt which is all that we can know. Lena, *Skipstone*, John, the prostheses, the dead themselves cannot become other than what they are but must only recapitulate themselves over and again. Trapped within the consciousness of the writer, the penitentiary of his being, much as the writer himself has been trapped within the *Skipstone* of his mortality, Lena and her dead emerge.

They emerge into a known sector of the universe.

And this is where they are.

XLIX

They emerge in the year 1975, July 1975, in the town of Ridge-field Park, New Jersey, floating to the cobbled and bleak surfaces of that town in a haze which absorbs all matter and there, by the laws of energy conservation and probability, they come to inhabit the bodies of the fifteen thousand souls of that town. They merge with them, become part of their consciousness so that they cannot be distinguished, they assume not only the flesh but the persona, the jobs, the loves and lives and memories of the residents of this little town, and there they remain and there they will be. There they are; there they are now.

And now and now and yet and yet: dwelling, amidst the refineries, strolling on Main Street past the Rialto Theatre, queuing at the theater to see films at reduced prices, shopping in the supermarkets, pausing in the gas stations, pairing off and clutching one another, some of them, in the imploded stars of their beds at the very moment at which the author, that cosmic accident himself, writes this about them.

Yes, it seems unimaginable that they would come, Lena and the dead, from the heart of the black galaxy to reconstruct and tenant the town of Ridgefield Park, New Jersey . . . but there is something less imaginable which makes, finally, this difficult resolution just for all.

For how can this be? How can it be? That from all the Ridgefield Parks of our time we will assemble to build the great engines which will take us to the stars . . . and some of the stars will bring death and others will bring life and then there are those which will bring us nothing at all, but the engines will continue, they will go on forever.

And so, in a fashion, after our fashion, will we.

GALAXIES

ABOUT THE AUTHOR

BARRY N. MALZBERG is an American writer, editor, and agent. His prolific career has spanned numerous genres, most notably crime and science fiction. Malzberg was particularly active in the SF scene of the early seventies, although he became disillusioned with the market forces defining the field and has rarely published SF works since. His most recent activity in the field has been in the form of advice columns for writers in the quarterly magazine of the Science Fiction and Fantasy Writers of America. Malzberg won the first John W. Campbell Memorial Award for *Beyond Apollo* in 1973. Over the years, his writing has been shortlisted for the Hugo, Nebula, and Philip K. Dick Awards, among others.

OTHER AOP TITLES